I-Waggit
The Titans of Tartarus

M. G. Sunderland

Quadsoft Books LLC

ISBN-13: 9798710199930
ISBN-10: 1477123456

Library of Congress Control Number: 2018675309
Printed in the United States of America

CONTENTS

PREFACE

Sergeant Waggit entered the wormhole and began his journey to the original Galaxy that he was from known as the Milky Way Galaxy. Along his journey through the wormhole, Sergeant Waggit discovered a malfunction within his ship that caused him to be stranded in a Void out in the middle of space with no light visible for millions of miles. With carefully configuring the spaceship's design and understanding how everything works within the electronics of the dash and the engine management system, Sergeant Waggit took it upon himself to repair the ship as he was the only one there. During his stay in the middle of the Void, Sergeant Waggit became Looney with his vision and dreams as he kept dozing off and dreaming of a stellar attack upon his ship even though there was absolutely nothing there.

Once Sergeant Waggit had finally repaired the ship and was ready to activate the gravity drive system to create the wormhole and continue his path, a rogue form hole came out in the middle of nowhere. Sergeant Waggit tried to redirect the position of his spaceship but knew that at that point it was too late. He literally had to force the spaceship into the wormhole and hoping that wherever he was going to be going was going to be his direction. However, right at the very last second, Sergeant Waggit was able to activate the gravity drive system just as the ship entered into this rogue warm hole allowing the ship to pass through double warm holes at the same time. This time while traveling through a double wormhole, Sergeant Waggit was conscious and was able to see exactly what he missed while he was passed out previously when he was aboard the Singularity.

After exiting the wormhole, the ship was in position of the solar system where planet Earth would resign. However, the planet earth and its Moon for that matter was missing and the other planets were in place however they were in a different type of orbit around the sun. Sergeant Waggit operated the newly specified platform built in the spaceship that was designed for time travel. After a moment, a flashlight occurred and then all of a sudden the ship arrived when the planet earth and its moon was existent within the solar system. Not knowing of the exact location of where the ship was placed at made it a difficult pathway to enter airspace of Earth. Sergeant Waggit had to divert the spacecraft as it was on a collision course with the Moon.

Once the spaceship was out of the lunar surface of the Moon and entered the airspace of

Earth, Sergeant Waggit put in the location within the navigation system to find the most important object of all time, the Rod of God. Upon landing and a remote location within Romania, the ship took up a heavy burden and crash landed causing the engines to suck up a lot of soil and dirt. When the engines were restarted, a very large explosion occurred which could be visible for miles. Using his suit as a disguise within the planet Earth making himself look like the people among the lands, Sergeant Waggit adapted his uniform to look like a farmer, security officer, a woman, and a professional business personnel.

Once discovering the location of the Rod of God, Sergeant Waggit noticed a couple of Russian soldiers that had taken the relic and boarded an aircraft to flee from Romania to the United States. Sergeant Waggit followed the soldiers in another aircraft that was heading from Romania to the United States but encountered something that was extremely horrific. While I'm bored the flight, Sergeant Waggit witnessed some hijackers taking the plane over with a bomb in the cargo department. using his suit to transform into other personnel within the flight making him disguised as everyone and having the help of a stewardess, Sergeant Waggit was able to take control of the aircraft but had to make a crash landing in New York.

After the aircraft was down and everyone was rescued that was on board, Sergeant Waggit noticed the soldiers were fleeing from the other aircraft that landed before them and tried to make a break for it with the relic in their hands. Sergeant Waggit took it upon himself to go after the Russian soldiers but in doing so literally tore apart the airport piece by piece to get the relic out of the Russian's hands. The chase led from the airport to the nearby waters making it even more difficult for Sergeant Waggit to secure the relic. After a very long brutal battle of trying to capture the Russian soldiers and retain the relic from their hands on the waters, the Russian soldiers managed to get away. Sergeant Waggit was not going to let them off that easy by applying a blow dart to the last soldier that boarded their craft which had a microchip within its housing that allowed Sergeant Waggit to track their location.

While Sergeant Waggit was captured by the nearby Coast Guard which imprisoned him in one of their camps that was south of New York. Of course having the ability to transform into anyone, Sergeant Waggit uses his abilities to transform into a janitor and then a pilot which in turn he was able to escape from the hands of the Coast Guard. Sergeant Waggit headed out to catch another flight in Denver, Colorado, which by him diverting the aircraft as a remote flown in, and by transferring his body into a businessman figure, Sergeant Waggit font that he was in the clear and was able to leave the country to Russia. However,

Sergeant Waggithad no idea that he was going to be placed in the same room and same location within the airport of his earlier self. After talking to his earlier self and trying to warn him of particular events that were going to happen soon, Sergeant Waggit showed his true identity to his original self but had no idea his original self was going to betray his trust.

Once Sergeant Waggit was airborne and in route to Russia to discover the location of where the relic was, the president of the United States aboard Air Force One, made a deal with Sergeant Waggit to be a secret spy for the U.S. Upon agreement of being a secret spy, Sergeant Waggit was able to clearly see what was happening within the dwellings of an underground secret laboratory beneath a prison compound in Russia. During his tour through the caverns and sub-levels beneath the surface of the prison camp, Sergeant Waggit noticed that in the living quarters a Russian soldier, which fit the description from the video that he had recorded from when he was in Romania, ran out of a room at which a fireball was following him. Sergeant Waggit headed into the room not to find just the relic, known as the Rod of God, on a table, but rather to find a creature that was thought just to be a myth. The creature by the name of Shaft, which was a demon-like creature similar to the Grim Reaper but was a woman in figure, attacked Sergeant Waggit so he would not be able to get the relic. Once the firefight was near the end and the Rod of God was in Sergeant Waggit's hands, Shaft took it upon herself and ripped away the stones that were in a pouch among Sergeant Waggit's waist. Before he could do anything about the current situation, Sergeant Waggit knew that it was too late and now knows that these stones are somewhere in the underworld.

After leaving the underground military installation within a prison compound, Sergeant Waggit was detained by the United States military and transferred to the Pentagon where he was to be imprisoned and questioned for his unwillingness behavior during his work as a spy. Of course without a doubt, Sergeant Waggit broke out of the most secure prison in the entire world by portraying to be other people as he was able to transform. After his victory of being escaped, Sergeant Waggit fled on a bus to keep a low profile all the way down to Houston, Texas, where he would meet up with the crew that was about to board a shuttle to fly up to the newly created ship in space known as the Singularity. Sergeant Waggit secretly boarded the space shuttle so no one would know he was there and also the same matter on the Singularity as well. After traveling through the space and witnessing all the events all over again that Sergeant Waggit revisioned, the crew then was sent back to Earth which now was considered one hundred seventy years later from the time they left. After a short while, a spacecraft from the Andromeda Galaxy entered the airspace of the Earth and caused all kinds of complex issues to all the militaries worldwide. Once a war broke out between the people of the Earth and the people of the Andromedan race, Sergeant Waggit took it upon himself to become a new superhero to the world and eliminate the threat that was going to destroy the planet by deflecting a giant rocket back into space.

As the Earth was now considered safe and no longer on a destruction path, Sergeant Waggit knew that he needed to get on his pathway to finding the Rod of God. Having spoken to many people on the streets and searching multiple different libraries, Sergeant Waggit discovered the secret location entry to the underworld which was also known as Tartarus. By holding the rod of God high above his head in the dark sky on Halloween night with a blue moon in the waters of the Mediterranean Sea near Crete, Sergeant Waggit was able to open the entryway to Tartarus. Sergeant Waggit entered the entryway, which was a very large archway that had some kind of a glow effect to it. The entryway led Sergeant Waggit to Tartarus which is also known for the underground depths of Hell. Sergeant Waggit fell through a wormhole that was full of stars flying by at extreme speeds that led him to the underworld which the only way to return is to obtain the stones that are missing.

CHAPTER ONE

Caverns of the Deep

Sergeant Waggit after falling down from exiting the wormhole into the lands of Tartarus. He looked around, saw his current location, and wanted to know what was lurking near him. The air was breathable and clearer than anywhere on Earth. The walls that surround the area were full of nothing but moss and moisture that could cause a dramatic smell in the future if it was to dry out. The ground was dripping with water from the ceiling as if there was some form of river above or a basin that had lots of body of water. Reaching down to touch the water on the floor, Sergeant Waggit soon realized that it was not water at all but rather some form of liquid that made his hand begin to tingle as if it was like acid or something. Everything was looking just like a cavern down in a deep tunnel underground or a form of cave. Sergeant Waggit reached over to his shoulder and activated the cloaking mechanism to transform himself back into his Andromedans form that the suit was originally created to look like. Then he began his journey walking through the caverns looking for the stones that were taken from him. There were many types of different bushes and flowery objects that looked devouring to want to eat but could be extremely poisonous. As he was walking along through the thick waters on the ground, Sergeant Waggit heard his little splashing sound that was coming from one of the nearby puddles and decided to walk over to it to examine the puddle. All of a sudden the flashing of the puddle stopped dead still as if something new that someone was standing right next to the puddle gave a good indication to be hidden. Sergeant Waggit couldn't bear it anymore and had to reach down into the puddle to feel what was in there as he thought it could be some kind of a creature or maybe something else. Despite his curiosity within the depths of the underground world within, Sergeant Waggit had no idea what was about to jump out at him and scare the living tarnation out of him.

As Sergeant Waggit put his hand into the Mercury liquid that was lying within the grounds of the floor that he was standing nearby, a little tiny creature came out hanging on to his index finger. The little creature looked just like a little miniature demon, which was red in color, and had little miniature horns on his head with tiny hooves for feet. The little miniature demon though was very cute and had these gorgeous eyes and a gorgeous little face that was undeniable to look at. The little demon really light was hanging on Sergeant Waggit's index finger as if it was a safe haven location from anything else within the underworld. Sergeant Waggit found that this new little demon could be his servant or pet that would be his friend to keep him completely sane. reaching down and petting the little demon made the demon very curious of the feel and touch expressing itself with a big grin on his face and luscious eyes shining within the minimal light that was within the caverns. Sergeant Waggit said to the little demon, "Hey little guy, what is your name or should I name you?" The little demon did absolutely nothing except make a little tiny bit of a grunting sound with a gulp. The sound was as if it was a miniature little dinosaur from back in the day just staring at somebody with no vocals whatsoever to make any kind of other sound other than the sound of a grunt. Sergeant Waggit looked at the little demon and said while petting it, "I will call you... Furfur." The little demon perked up his ears and tilted his head with a big luscious smile and gleaming eyes as it heard the name "Furfur" being said in a most graceful way. then the little demon decided that it wanted to run all over the place and run up Sergeant Waggit's arm and all around his entire suit until it landed on his shoulder sitting there like if it was a little bird on a pirate's shoulder. Sergeant Waggit looked over at his shoulder and saw the little demon sitting there with a Little grunt and pointing towards the forward direction in front of him. Sergeant Waggit looked at the little demon and said, "Alright, we will get a move on and continue our search for the stones that I am missing."

Sergeant Waggit continued his research while he was walking through the caverns that were within the deep tunnels of the underground within Tartarus. Along the way traveling through the caverns, Sergeant Waggit encountered a dead soldier that had a unique rifle attached to his shoulder. Beside the rifle was an ammunition can full of magazines that were loaded and ready for any conflict. Without a hesitation, Sergeant Waggit picked up the rifle and the box of ammunition. The side of the rifle had a saying on it in ancient Hebrew that said, "Heavy Cannon Rifle". Also, nearby the soldier, Sergeant Waggit found a strap that had thirty grenades that were to be used by the rifle. He picked up the strap and wrapped it around his left shoulder. After walking for many steps that ended up being lots of miles that he had covered, Sergeant Waggit came across some unusual mushrooms that were growing on the walls. To his curiosity, Sergeant Waggit could not resist the temptation of the mushrooms and had to take one for himself. Sergeant Waggit took out a blade that he had within his pouch and sliced one of the mushrooms off the walls. after reaching down and picking up the mushroom that had landed on the floor from cutting it off the wall, Sergeant Waggit tried sharing the mushroom with the little demon but the little demon refused by shaking its head back and forth indicating that it did not want it with a little grunt at the same time. Then the most irresponsible thing happened that Sergeant Waggit did as the taste of the mushroom must have been most desirable as he shoved it down his throat. And of course just like anyone that ingests something that is not actually made for your body could possibly have some interesting side effects. At first, Sergeant Waggit was feeling absolutely normal and then all of a sudden he started feeling as if the walls were coming in on him. Then the ceiling was falling down towards his location making him feel as if the room was getting smaller and smaller. Sergeant Waggit felt like the walls and ceiling were actually moving and that he needed to figure out a way out of there as quickly as possible so he would not be trapped or squished to an oblivion. The room began to change colors as if Sergeant Waggit was looking through a kaleidoscope. There word numerous different types of spectrum colors and angled designs that kept rotating and its manual fashion direction. Running as fast as he could through the caverns of the deep, Sergeant Waggit ran all the way down a hallway towards a light that was near the end. At the last second right when Sergeant Waggit reached the light, he simply reached out and tried to pull the light down but noticed that the light fell and broke into a million pieces as if it was actually a light bulb that was lit up. To his surprise, Sergeant Waggit thought that he was standing outside of the underground caverns and saw a huge set of steps that would lead him to somewhere that he doesn't really know of. Taking each step by step dragging his feet across each one as the steps are extremely tall, to be exactly of over three feet in diameter, Sergeant Waggit used as much breath as he possibly could breathing in very difficult times until he had reached the most top of the staircase. Once he was at the very top, Sergeant Waggit noticed that there was absolutely nothing up there except a staircase to go back down and he thought to himself, "What was the fuck'n purpose of climbing those stairs?" Then Sergeant Waggit decided to head down the stairs in the opposite direction that he came up but then his foot slipped and allowed him to roll all the way down. Seeing nothing but sky and land and sky and land over and over made Sergeant Waggit feel sick to himself but had no idea that the reason why he was feeling sick had nothing to do with tumbling but more of the mushrooms taking over his insanity.

After lying down on the ground for quite some time to be exact for more than three days, Sergeant Waggit woke up and looked around to see where exactly he was. He noticed that the light was actually a lantern that he had ripped off the wall and smashed it all over the ground spewing lantern oil everywhere. The staircase that Sergeant Waggit thought that he was climbing was nothing more than logs that were piled up near a fireplace within the caverns. The fireplace was extremely tall and full of wood that was burning, keeping a nice warmth within the area that Sergeant Waggit was lying within. He said to himself as he was staring at the fireplace, "I know that this fireplace is here and that it was not here before. I know I would have seen the light from it or was this all just a dream." The little demon on his shoulder pointed towards the top of the fireplace and grunted with a big gulp. Sergeant Waggit concerningly looked up at the top of the fireplace to see nothing but a gargoyle staring at him. At first, Sergeant Waggit thought that the gargoyle was nothing but a statue that was crafted and placed there to scare off any personnel that dares to sit near the fireplace, but rather the gargoyle was not a statue and indeed it was actually real as it blinked its eyes at him. Sergeant Waggit, feeling like a chicken took off like a bat out of hell running down the hallway once again. the little demon literally had to grab his uniform and hold on for dear life as wind was passing across him at great speeds as Sergeant Waggit was running completely scared out of his mind. At the very last second, Sergeant Waggit ran into a wall which made him bounce off and land on the floor knocking him out cold. After a few moments the little demon took its tongue and smacked it into his right ear. Sergeant Waggit could not bear the feeling of having something wet in his ear and like if it was a wet willy and he did nothing but stand up and scream at the top as lungs, "Aaawwwwe!!!"

The little demon turned around on Sergeant Waggit's shoulder and then began to grunt horrendously back and forth. Sergeant Waggit then said to the little demon, "Oh, there's something behind me, isn't there." The little demon grunted twice indicating that he was acknowledging Sergeant Waggit's statement. Sergeant Waggit turned around and saw nothing was standing behind him whatsoever. There was a creature that was there standing behind him but as Sergeant Waggit turned around it vanished as quickly as possible to get right behind him again. Next to Sergeant Waggit was a pitchfork that was resting up against the wall. Sergeant Waggit reached out and very slowly put a good firm grip around the handle of the Pitchfork and at the very last second of making his thought process, Sergeant Waggit took the Pitchfork and swung it as fast as he could as he turned around. The pitch for pierced flesh of a beautiful woman that was standing right behind him. the woman began to gas as the fork appeared to her belly spewing blood out. Along with her gasping, the woman also started gulping as she was feared she was to die from the pitchfork stuck in her flesh. Sergeant Waggit let go of the Pitchfork and said to the woman, "I... I'm so sorry that I didn't realize that such beauty was standing behind me." The woman then looks indirectly into the eyes of Sergeant Waggit, as if she was staring directly into his soul. Then unspeakable happened as the woman began to start laughing horrendously at Sergeant Waggit. The woman continued to laugh louder and louder and more of a screeching sound at near the end. Then the Pitchfork fell to the ground as the woman's body merely turned into nothing but dark ash. Sergeant Waggit thought to himself, "What the fuck is this place?" Then in the corner of his eyes, Sergeant Waggit saw some kind of a doorway at the end of the hall. He began to wander down the hallway to the door that would lead him to somewhere of the unknown. Opening the door within the hallway of the underground cavern that led Sergeant Waggit on a goose chase, was nothing but another cavern but this time it had a different outtake.

This new cavern that Sergeant Waggit was standing within was red in color and had unique markings along pillars that were holding up the ceiling. The markings were similar to what you would find in Medusa's lair but rather vertical drawings instead of horizontal drawings. Also there was a missed amongst the floor that covered the ground to where you could not see where you were stepping. Along with the mist was crumbles of rock that would sometimes fall from the sides under the ground indicating that either some unnatural thing was causing the rock to fall or there was something like an earthquake making it fall.

In the far distance of the caverns was a fiery type of light which in turn could be another fireplace but this light was more of a miniature sun. Alongside of the fiery light was a huge black creature that was standing there staring at the light with its back towards Sergeant Waggit. Having great ambitions of what was going to happen next, Sergeant Waggit had to seek out the black creature as if it could have been Shaft, the creature from the other realm that took his stones. Sergeant Waggit ran through the caverns as fast as he could and as soon as he got to the block creature, the creature turned around and smacked him upside the head with a giant ax. While laying on the ground, Sergeant Waggit was slightly inferior; this creature raised its ax high up in the air and was getting ready to swing it down and penetrate his armor. Then, the little demon that was on Sergeant Waggit's shoulder ran down to his chest and grunted at the black creature. While throwing his ax behind him, the black creature stepped back as he was frightened by the little demon. Then he forced himself into the ball of fire which then made himself disappear from existence. Sergeant Waggit was shocked to see that such a large creature was scared of something so tiny but had no idea what the purpose of the little demon really was.

Sergeant Waggit got up and continued his journey through the underground caverns within the deep darkness of Tartarus. Along the way,

Sergeant Waggit saw a really unique table set that was all destroyed, broken down, upside down, and burned as if they were part of some kind of a ship or scene. While Sergeant Waggit was staring at the table set, the most bizarre thing began to happen. The table set then began to clean itself and reconstruct itself back to its original state as if nothing had happened. Then Sergeant Waggit was standing in a dance hall that was full of people cheering him on indicating that he had done something very graceful. Sergeant Waggit's favorite band of all time was ACDC. He looked at the microphone where the stage was being reconstructed in the room that he was standing in and saw the lead singer, Bon Scott, staring at him with a really ratified cool look. With an astonished look on his face, Sergeant Waggit was excited to see his favorite band on a stage in the underworld of Tartarus. Bon Scott walked off the stage and headed right over to Sergeant Waggit to greet him with a firm handshake. As Bon Scott reached out to shake the hand of Sergeant Waggit, there was a strange feeling that it was applied within Sergeant Waggit's chest. With little to no fear, Sergeant Waggit reached out and shook the hand of Bon Scott. Sergeant Waggit then saw the hand turn into fire which in turn the entire body of Bon Scott burst into flames. Sergeant Waggit tried to let go of the firm handshake but was unable to as the grass was immensely strong. There was extreme heat pouring upon his chest plate causing it to begin heating up as if there was a boiler pumping steam against it. Sergeant Waggit took out a knife that was in his pouch and used it to slice off the arm that was attached to the firm handshake. The hand then released and fell to the ground which burned into ash along with the rest of the body falling to the ground into ash. Sergeant Waggit then said to himself, "This place is becoming extremely weird and I do know that they don't want me here for some reason. My past keeps revisiting myself while I'm down here along with strange anomalies that keep occurring. I just need to hurry the fuck up and find those damn stones."

Sergeant Waggit then headed down the rest of the way through the caverns within the deep underneath the ground in Tartarus. He discovered that there was an icy slope at the end of the tunnel that he was in and had to figure out a way to find an exit. Trying to jump across the icy slope onto another area that was like a platform that he could grab onto would be merely a coincidence if Sergeant Waggit could make the jump. Sergeant Waggit stepped back a little bit, positioned himself for a proper take off, and then took off running as fast as he could to make a very large leap across the icy slope. After flying through the air lunging from one platform to another, Sergeant Waggit was able to make it to the other side. However, after standing on the other platform across from the icy slope, the ground gave out making Sergeant Waggit fall and land onto the icy slope. Now, Sergeant Waggit was sliding down an icy slope that seemed like it went on forever. Sergeant Waggit tried to grab onto something while sliding down the ice slope but could not hold the grass as he was going too fast. At the end of the icy slope in a far distance ahead, Sergeant Waggit could see something that was large, tall, and white. His intentions were to get out of the area but do it in a safe manner without destroying himself or the little creature that mattered that is hanging on to his shoulder for dear life. The very large white mountain-like structure became closer and closer as Sergeant Waggit continued to slide down the slope at astonishing speeds. Then right at the very last second just before Sergeant Waggit would come in contact with the White mountain-like structure, Sergeant Waggit noticed that the structure was a huge amount of snow, which could blanket his fall causing him to be cushioned. With speeds up to sixty miles per hour, Sergeant Waggit slammed into the snow mound, slowing him down to an absolute zero speed.

Sergeant Waggit used all of his might to climb out of the snow mound. Once he was standing outside of the snowman looking at an exit that was nearby, Sergeant Waggit noticed that his little demon friend-like creature that was on his shoulder was absolutely frozen to the crisp. Sergeant Waggit remembered that he had a bunch of hand warmers that were in his pouch, so he cracked one open and placed it between the legs of the little demon that was standing on his shoulder. The little heat packet began to heat up the creature and slowly melted away the frosty ice that was built up around its body. Soon after the heat warmer applied to the body of the little demon, a grunting sound began to occur and Sergeant Waggit turned his head to see if that was coming from the little demon. Sergeant Waggit saw that the little demon was okay at the moment and asked him, "Are you okay little buddy?" The little demon reached his right hand out and gave a thumbs up for Sergeant Waggit to see, indicating that he was good to go as any other day. Sergeant Waggit then headed towards the exit that he saw that led him to an outdoor area that looked like a forest.

CHAPTER TWO

Forest in the Swamp

Just on the outside of the caverns was a land that was completely full of green vegetated trees. Along with the trees was mass amounts of salt water along with tremendous amounts of different types of insects. There was rotting vegetation, dripping trees with black trunks, and a thick quicksand that is lurking within the shadowy areas of the water. The ground had a mist applied to it. It looked like some form of fog but yet it was more of a toxic gas that was carbon dioxide in nature. The smell of gas bubbles rising through the water was strong similar to a rotting carcass and decaying sweat glands from trees. The air had a nasty taste as if you were drinking stale water from a canteen or if you were eating food that was from a can that's over expired from years before. Due to the climate and the moisture in the air, Sergeant Waggit had his uniform sticking to his body and as he stepped down into the mud, water began seeping into his boots causing his feet to become extremely muddy and clumpy which began to stick to his skin.

Sergeant Waggit knew that he was not just standing on some kind of forest but it was more of a very large disgusting swamp. He continued walking through the thick muddy water in the search for any stones that he could find that were missing. The little demon on Sergeant Waggit's shoulder was shivering in fear as he knew that there could be something nearby that might cause harm to the both of them. As he continued his path through the deep waters, Sergeant Waggit saw something poke it an eye out of the water and then plunge back down and to the darkness shadows that lurk below the water. Sergeant Waggit looked at the little demon and said, "Did you see that shit little guy?" The little demon clenched up in a small ball with his fingers in his mouth chomping on his fingernails and terrified fear looked over at Sergeant Waggit and granted with a slight smile upon his face and gave him a thumbs up. Sergeant Waggit moved forward through the water and again the creature that worked within the deep dark shadows pumped another eyeball up out of the water and looked directly at Sergeant Waggit. Then the eye plunged back down into the darkness and floating nearby was a little body of a creature that was unknown. The eyeball then popped out of the water right in front of Sergeant Waggit which caused him to pull out his knife and/ at the eye making it come off of whatever it was attached to falling back into the deep of the water.

The creature that the eye was attached to screamed underneath the water in tears and pain. Then without any warning signs, the creature stood straight out of the water towering over Sergeant Waggit. The creature was about twelve feet tall and looked like a giant praying mantis with long arms that had tree limbs attached to the end of it. On top of its head there were marshlands of grass and grum that would allow the creature to disguise itself as part of the grassy knoll that was within the swampy water. The color of the creature was in two different types of green to be precise of lime green and OD green blending into the swamp water. The creature looked directly into the eyes of the little demon that was on Sergeant Waggit's shoulder and began to grunt at it as if it was trying to communicate with the little demon. The little demon then grunted back and put a thumbs down as if it did not want to talk to this creature whatsoever. Sergeant Waggit didn't know whether this creature was there to attack or if it was just simply another guide, however, the creature was quite disturbing to look at and had a good sense that it was going to attack Sergeant Waggit as he slashed one of its eyes off. Sergeant Waggit took out his big rifle and pointed it at the creature. The creature took this as a sign that Sergeant Waggit was going to attack it and attempt to attack him by lunging directly towards his location. By squeezing the trigger of the rifle, Sergeant Waggit blasted a grenade directly at the creature.

When the grenade hit the creature, it caused the creature to blow into pieces. The remainder of the body fell to the ground dropping down into the deep waters of the darkness.

Right after the creature fell into the marsh waters of the deep dark swamp, Sergeant Waggit heard a noise within the waters that sounded like more of these creatures were heading his direction. The water was making a ripple effect as if there were multiple amounts of creatures heading directly to his location. The little demon was so feared that he might die as these creatures are going to do a massive attack. Sergeant Waggit locked and loaded his rifle and was ready to attack any of them that were going to lunge at him. Once the creatures were nearby the water ripples stopped moving giving the illusion that the creatures either left or they completely stopped in their tracks. Then without a warning, each creature lunged out of the water as quickly as it could heading directly at Sergeant Waggit. Without any hesitation, Sergeant Waggit began unleashing hell with his rifle upon every single creature blasting them back to the underworld that they came from. Sergeant Waggit yelled out as he was shooting each creature one by one, "Fuck you!!... Die motherfucker!!... Oh, you want some too!! Fuck you!!" After wasting seven rounds of grenades and a half clip of magazine within the rifle, all the creatures were now dead and floating amongst the dark waters of the swamplands. Sergeant Waggit looked at the little demon and said, "Now, that's how you paint the water red little guy." The little demon grunted while showing a gratitude expression on his little tiny cute face and gave two thumbs up while staring at Sergeant Waggit.

Continuing his voyage through the swamplands that look like a giant forest, Sergeant Waggit came across that mountain that he could climb up onto to get out of the water. Once he was on top of the mountain and held onto a tree branch that was near the edge, Sergeant Waggit felt the ground move a little bit. He took out his rifle and shot around into the ground that was underneath him. After blasting around to the ground the ground began to move even more with a humming noise. Sergeant Waggit looked at the little demon that was on his shoulder and said, "I think that the ground is alive. Don't you think, little guy." The little demon nodded and grunted in agreement with the ground moving as it could be alive. Sergeant Waggit could not hold his grip anymore and fell down the mountain rolling all the way down to the ground. While staring at the mountain, the mountain began to rise off the ground becoming very tall with four legs underneath it. With an extreme surprise look on his face, Sergeant Waggit could not believe that that mountain was a very large creature. He said to himself, "If this creature decides to attack me and my little friend here, just how and what the fuck am I supposed to do." The creature looks like a giant four-legged servant with two different mouths upon its head. The top mouth looked more like some form of alien creature and had razor sharp teeth with drool dropping off drizzling down through the marsh grasslands upon its back. The bottom set of teeth was surrounded by four different types of horns or giant teeth that stuck straight out of its body. There were no eyes to be found anywhere amongst the creature indicating that it either sensed smell or heat signatures to get around. The creature lowered its head down towards Sergeant Waggit and opened both of its mouths making an awful loud roar shooting out spit, saliva, and dirt with grimmy guts from other creatures spreading all over the area. Sergeant Waggit pointed his rifle directly towards the creature. Then he changed his mind and swapped the rifle out for the Rod of God and pointed it towards the creature instead. The creature saw the Rod of God and then its mouths shut with a growling sound and began grunting along with the growling. The ground then began to shake as the creature turned around and started walking away from Sergeant Waggit. With a disturbing look on his face, Sergeant Waggit didn't understand why the creature turned around and left but he had a good assumption that the power within the Rod of God probably is what the creature sensed and knew that it was too powerful to fight up against.

Sergeant Waggit began to follow the colossal creature in the hopes to find the stones that were missing. With his continuation of his search, Sergeant Waggit discovered a mushroom-like little kingdom that was in a small village just up ahead. The Little kingdom looked like large mushrooms that were full of evil presence of red tarnished color beams within the dwellings of each mushroom. Curiosity is always at the greatest with Sergeant Waggit when it comes to strange unnatural living environments. He decided to embark on entering one of the mushroom-like kingdom homes. Walking up the staircase to enter a mushroom building was very unstable as the staircase was rotting. As Sergeant Waggit took step by step up the staircase, one of the steps broke through making him fall all the way down with his legs stuck in the staircase. He managed to get himself up and tried to be more careful as he was climbing to the top of the staircase to enter the mushroom kingdom building. Once Sergeant Waggit had reached the front door to the mushroom kingdom building, he knocked on the door to see if somebody would open it for him or something. However, there was absolute silence and nothing was there to greet his astonishing presence just outside the door. With a big blow of the buttstock to his weapon, Sergeant Waggit forged his way through the front door into the mushroom-like kingdom building. While inside the mushroom-like kingdom building, Sergeant Waggit searched every inch by inch to see if he could locate any stones that were missing. There were many objects and obstacles that Sergeant Waggit had to overcome in order to continue his search. The building was much bigger than anticipated when standing outside. The stem of the building had a spiral staircase that went all the way down to the underground beneath the mushroom building. Sergeant Waggit with a little cute demon on his shoulder went down the spiral staircase to see if there was anything within the building that could show any signs of the missing stones. Once he was down beneath the building there was a long channel underneath the ground that traveled between that building to another building. Sergeant Waggit walked about the channel until he saw another staircase, which led him into another mushroom-like kingdom building. This second building was entertaining in a way to where some of the doors were locked that required a special type of key to open it. Sergeant Waggit tried to budge the door open but when the door did actually open it slammed shut and some sort of spell cast upon it with some lettering on the door. The words spelled out, "You must have a small skull key in order to open this door." Sergeant Waggit saw that maybe within the dwellings of that room that there could be a Stone lying on the open or placed in some magical box or chest of some sort. In order to continue his search, Sergeant Waggit had to go back down into the channel that was underneath the mushroom-like kingdom and find another mushroom-like building. With traveling due east, Sergeant Waggit ran into another staircase that led him up to a third mushroom-like building. Once inside the third building, Sergeant Waggit was able to perform a sweep throughout the entire dwellings of the walls in the search for the stones. While searching, Sergeant Waggit came across a red small skull key, which he picked up and placed into his small pouch that he was carrying. He thought about it for a moment and then realized that the other door he was at didn't have any kind of a color whatsoever but rather just a small skunky instead. Sergeant Waggit then said to himself, "Maybe this keep belongs to something else and could be used to unlock either a door chest or cabinet of some sort that may just have what I'm looking for."

Sergeant Waggit headed back down the staircase and into the channel. This time headed due west across the plain of the channel in the hopes of finding a fourth mushroom-like building. Instead of finding a staircase that goes up, Sergeant Waggit found a staircase that went down indicating that there could be a secret chamber underneath the channel that he was walking through. Sergeant Waggit took the staircase that went down and followed it to wherever it was going to lead him. Halfway down the staircase there was a gate that was marked with a yellow color stone upon the top of it with glowing eyes. Sergeant Waggit took out the yellow key that he had found in the other mushroom-like building and put it into the gates lock. With a quick turn the locking mechanism to the gates lock was released and the gate swung open. After stepping through the gate, Sergeant Waggit continued heading down the staircase as it was going on for a very long time. Then at the very last moment of walking down the staircase, Sergeant Waggit finally reached the end which led him into another channel underneath the ground. This second channel took him all the way to a giant old looking chest, which looked like something an old ancient burial ship left this chest full of gold or something like as it was a trap for pirates. There was a key slot in the chest but no color identification or anything to signify what kind of key is required to open it. Sergeant Waggit opened his pouch and retrieved the small skull key and put it into the locking mechanism within the large chest. Unfortunately the key did not work and left Sergeant Waggit puzzled once again. Sergeant Waggit then turned around and headed back through the lower channel and back up the long tall staircase to the upper channel. He saw a crack in the wall along the channel and decided to take the buttstock of his weapon and slam it against the crack. Rubbish of all kinds of dirt, bones, and debris fell down exposing a secret hideout or another channel that could be heading toward the north direction. Sergeant Waggit entered this new chamber and followed it all the way down to where there was another staircase heading up to another mushroom-like building. When he entered the building, Sergeant Waggit searched everywhere to locate if there was a possible way of finding his stones or another key for that matter. Then it was the most unspeakable bizarre thing he ever saw in the underworld. A box came out of a closet with wings on it flapping around. The box had a mouth with eyes and it kept saying, with repeating itself over and over and over, "You shall be drained of all your power if you open me to unlock the tower." Sergeant Waggit tried to catch the box but the box was too fast as it kept flapping around in the high most of the mushroom-like building like if it was a bat of some sort. Then just with curiosity, Sergeant Waggit decided to harness his rifle and take out the Rod of God. He pointed the rod directly towards the box and said, "Drop. I command you to drop now." At first nothing happened and it seemed like the rod wasn't going to do anything for Sergeant Waggit at all. Then all of a sudden a burst of energy blasted out of the end of the rod casting it onto the box. The energy wrapped around the box causing it to be within the grasp of the energies binding voltage. Sergeant Waggit moved the rod up and down and noticed that the box moved with it. So, Sergeant Waggit moved the rod down as quickly as he could, causing the box to slam onto the ground breaking in a million pieces. Once the box was broken, Sergeant Waggit walked over to it and noticed that there was a small skull that was shiny like gold inside the broken box. He picked up the shiny skull that was golden in color and put it into his pouch as he could possibly need it sometime in the future.

Sergeant Waggit searched the mushroom-like building to see if there was anything else that could be hiding within the rooms. After his search, Sergeant Waggit headed out of the mushroom-like building down the staircase back into the channel. He then walked all the way down the channel and saw another wall that had a bunch of cracks on it. Again using his buttstock, Sergeant Waggit broke down the wall allowing the rubbish to fall down onto the floor of the channel exposing a short narrow hallway that had a little line at the other end. With a huge mind of curiosity, Sergeant Waggit had to go down the short little hallway to seek out the light. As Sergeant Waggit became near to the light, he noticed that it was not just a light but more of a torch that was attached to the side of the hallway. there was a wall on the other side that had lines around it but no entryway of any kind and it was unable to be destroyed either. Sergeant Waggit thought about it for a moment and then discovered that if he was to pull down onto the torch then maybe something would happen. Sergeant Waggit reached out and grabbed the bottom of the torch and pulled it down. The wall that had the lines around it began to move and rotated sideways and then stopped. Another hallway was exposed through the doorway that just opened up that led to another mushroom-like building that was nearby. Sergeant Waggit walked sideways and entered this other hallway that he just unrevealed and as soon as he passed the doorway, Sergeant Waggit stepped on a stone that was on the ground causing the door to shut behind him. With nowhere to go except heading towards the mushroom-like building, Sergeant Waggit illuminated his flashlights that he had on his uniform and followed the path until it came to a staircase that was going up. Once he reached the staircase, Sergeant Waggit began to climb it until he reached the mushroom-like building. Sergeant Waggit saw that the building had a door that was locked; however inside the center of the door was a small hole that was just big enough to fit something inside it. He reached inside his pouch and took out the golden skull that he had recovered from the other mushroom-like building and he placed it into the hole within the door. All of a sudden there was a clunk sound and the door swung open. Sergeant Waggit entered the mushroom-like building with caution as there could be something there lurking about to attack him or take something from him.

Once inside the mushroom-like building, Sergeant Waggit began to walk around searching every inch looking for either the stones, a key, or some other type of object that would aid his way in finding the stones that he was looking for. In the back room of the mushroom-like building the door was shut and there were shadows of feet moving back and forth as if someone was pacing left and right from the door. Sergeant Waggit harnessed the Rod of God and slung out his rifle and was prepared for anything that was about to lurk at him. With a very large blow to the door in the back room, Sergeant Waggit was able to knock it open. Inside the back room was a mythical creature known as 'Minotaur' , a half man and half bull. The Minotaur stood a towering of 12 ft inside the room. In the left hand of the Minotaur there was a giant shield that could deflect anything except for fire. In the right hand of the Minotaur there was a long staff that was used to poke at the enemies that came near it. Sergeant Waggit didn't know that the shield would be considered as armor resistant and as he shot his rifle unloading an entire magazine full of rounds towards the creature, the rounds just kept bouncing off the shield as if it was being deflected along with the creature moving the shield in every direction dodging itself from every single bullet. Sergeant Waggit then harnessed his weapon and took out his Rod of God. He pointed the rod directly towards the creature and yelled out, "You shall die!" Then the rod blasted a fireball outside of the tip directly towards the shield that the Minotaur was holding. The fireball pierced the shield causing it to burn up into flames and reduce its size. Sergeant Waggit continued to allow the rod to fire more fireballs at the shield until the shield vanished from the Minotaur's hand. The Minotaur then took the staff that it was holding in its right hand and pointed it at Sergeant Waggit. With very big fast blow lunges, the Minotaur tried to attack Sergeant Waggit but with a blow from the rod to the staff several times, the Minotaur's staff broke in half. Now that the Minotaur was defenseless, Sergeant Waggit harnessed the Rod of God and took out his rifle. He fired an entire clip of rounds until the miniature was no longer standing and laying on the ground. Sergeant Waggit saw something hanging on the belt on the side of the Minotaur that was shiny like a new key. Slowly he reached down without knowing if the Minotaur would grab him or attack him again and retrieved the shiny object. The object that Sergeant Waggit took from the Minotaur was just another key, however, this key was larger and had a gold nugget within a silver bracket around the top. Sergeant Waggit thought to himself, "I wonder if this key will unlock the chest that I found in the other channel." Sergeant Waggit put the newly found key into his pouch and then searched the rest of the mushroom-like building for anything that he could find that would help him.

Once the sweep was completed, Sergeant

Waggit headed down the staircase back to the channel that he walked through. He headed back to the door that turned sideways and tried to activate it by stepping on the stone again. The stone clamps to the floor and a clunk sound sounded, however, the door did not budge. With a furious aggression raging through his teeth as he was grinding them, Sergeant Waggit grabbed the Rod of God and slammed it against the door as hard as he could. The power of the rod sent out a shockwave through the door causing it to shatter to pieces. Now that the door was no longer there Sergeant Waggit entered the other chamber that was on the other side and began his journey back to the staircase that went down. However, along the journey there was a covering over the staircase that was like a barrier of some kind of force field that would not allow him to go down it. Sergeant Waggit yelled out, "You have got to be shitting me!!" He then walked about the channel and saw some sort of bell that was hanging at a corner. Sergeant Waggit reached out and rang the bell making it have a cleaning sound. Shortly after the bell rang and echoed through the channel, the walls ground and top all began to shake horrendously. Once the shaking stopped, a goblin growling sound appeared within the channel. Sergeant Waggit slowly just to only see a dozen goblins standing behind him ready to pounce on him. Sergeant Waggit shouldered his Rod of God and grabbed his rifle with a quick snap. While pulling the trigger by his right index finger, rounds of ammunition began to spit out of the barrel blasting towards the goblins. Each round was encased with tipless explosives so when a came in contact with the goblins it literally shredded them. After destroying all twelve goblins the force field like structure that was keeping the underground channel blocked was now open. Sergeant Waggit ran down the channel and headed down the staircase as quickly as possible. Then he ran through the channel that was below and found the very large chest. Reaching into his pouch Sergeant Waggit pulled out the shiny key that had the gold nugget in it and stuck it into the locking mechanism of the chest. With a quick turn of the key the lock broke open allowing the top to be free to open up. Sergeant Waggit opened the chest and saw something bling within underneath a towel. He picked up the towel and saw that there was a stone underneath it. Sergeant Waggit remembered that he could not physically touch the stones by his hands and he had to use the special glove that was in his pocket. Sergeant Waggit reached into his pocket and took out the special glove. He put the glove on and reached out into the chest and with a quick grasp he picked up the stone. He then said to himself, "Well, I didn't get all of the stones but I did get one." Since Sergeant Waggit did not have the box to house the stones within, he decided to carve holes in the Rod of God to secure each stone. Then Sergeant Waggit dropped the first stone into the Rod of God. The stone then powered up the rod and gave it a unique color pattern indicating that the rod was accepting the power of the stone. The rod lit up with a cool light green color of lines all around it. Sergeant Waggit admired the cool looking rod that he was holding. Then he decided to turn the rod and look at the stone to determine which one he retrieved. To his acknowledgement, Sergeant Waggit had picked up the Chinook Stone. The stone had a cool dust cloud inside it. The power of the stone allowed the rod to create immense strong winds to cause the enemies to either rip apart or spin standing still allowing a deadly blow to be applied to them.

Sergeant Waggit headed towards the last mushroom-like building and went up the staircase and entered it. He then pointed the Rod of God towards a wall and touched the stone. The rod then came alive and channeled the power of the stone through it causing a huge wind to burst out and break through the wall. Sergeant Waggit was now free of the mushroom-like kingdom and was able to continue his journey in searching for the other stones as he only just found one. He said to himself as he was running past the mushroom-like kingdom, "If I had to fight a Minotaur to get a key to retrieve one of the stones, I wonder what I will have to fight next to get the next stone." Along the way past the mushroom-like kingdom, Sergeant Waggit found a double barrel shotgun that was lying on the ground. The powerful shotgun also had a box of rounds next to it. Sergeant Waggit secured the double barrel shotgun and the ammunition that came with it as he knew that the weapon may come in hand for what is about to come next.

CHAPTER THREE

The Dragon's Lair

Sergeant Waggit walked down a narrow path just passed the mushroom-like buildings and saw a dark cave just up ahead. The entrance to the cave was large and vigorous with hanging teeth like molds of rock. It was as if the entrance to the cave was similar to a giant mouth of a giant man eating worm. Sergeant Waggit got chills down the back of his neck as he saw blood dripping off the edges of the entryway to the cave. As he entered the massive cave Sergeant Waggit noticed that there were skeleton bones all over the place as if something either burned them alive or they were trapped forever. There was a stream that was flowing through the valley area within the cave that headed around a bend and into the abyss. Torches that were placed on the wall were existent of flame at the time and then all of a sudden within the flick of an eye the torch lit up blazing fast and strong with fire upon them. At that moment Sergeant Waggit could see everything within the cave for as far as that he could see the light anyway. He decided to follow the path of the waters to see where he would lead him as long as he didn't run into any troubles along the way. Without a notice, the ground started to shake and the walls began to tremble with rocks crumbling down the sides indicating that there was something large or a possible earthquake was occurring. Sergeant Waggit shielded himself from all of the debris that was falling from the ceiling onto the ground including very large boulders that would smash near him and in front and behind. One of the walls crumbled enough to where it left a little hole in it, big enough so that Sergeant Waggit could squeeze through and see what was just on the other side.

After passing through the wall hoping that nothing was left behind as the ground began to shake and blocked the pathway that was just entered, Sergeant Waggit was now in a secret room or part of the cave that revealed a dark past. Within the walls there were many markings that he could use his computer system to analyze to verify what they were. To his acknowledgment, Sergeant Waggit noticed that most of the markings on the walls were written in ancient Egyptian languages and were also many different types of constellations and some constellations that he had no idea of, maybe it was something that was created a long time ago and then destroyed. Mapping out all of the constellations led to a discovery knowing that the location where he was was indeed within the lands of Tartarus. Sergeant Waggit honestly thought that to Tartarus was a place within the depths of the grounds of hell on Earth. However, this was not the case as the land was nowhere near Earth to begin with. The land of Tartarus was in a vast location within space that belonged to a place called, 'Tarantula Nebula'. The Tarantula Nebula is the largest known nebula that is a stellar nursery which gives birth to new stars within the folds of gas and dust. A Black planet that circles the nebula's largest black hole is known as Tartarus. The planet is full of dark secrets and evil to the most impressive desire to destroy anything. Hades is the ruler of these lands within the underworld. The unknown constellations that Sergeant Waggit was looking at might have been located behind the nebula as it could be a star pattern for all existing life in multiple different directions. Other markings upon the walls were creatures that had bizarre outtakes to them. Some creatures were human in flesh but animatronic in design while other creatures were around and demon-like and could spit plasma or fireballs at anything that gets in their way. To add to the list, Sergeant Waggit noticed a drawing upon the walls carved with stone of a creature of unknown size really long and had two giant heads. While placing his hand onto the stone and feeling what it felt like, Sergeant Waggit could almost imagine what it would be like to fight such a monster. He thought to himself, "What would I be able to do if I were in the position to fight such a large disgusting fuck 'n monster."

Sergeant Waggit continued to search the room for multiple different other drawings that were on the walls and look at the paintings and everything that were amongst the ceiling. Some of the paintings on the ceiling were disturbing to look at as there was a single being shooting multiple weapons at a beast that was so immensely large and had multiple counter attacks. Other drawings within the ceiling showed multiple different demon-like creatures of different sizes. Some creatures would walk on two legs while other creatures would float in the air trying to bring all hell to every living existence object that is known.

A large Boulder was up against something that had a shine to it within the small section of the cave. Sergeant Waggit found a large stick that was on the ground made of some kind of old timber and used it to apply leverage to the boulder to make it roll off its current location. With the right applied leverage, the boulder slowly moved from its location revealing what it had pinned underneath. Shining bright in the room to Sergeant Waggit's eyes, was a bracelet that was shaped perfectly to fit around anyone's wrist and was made of gold with a red Jewel that had a tiny tornado inside it. as he made a huge Discovery within the cave and knew that something bad could happen if he did collect such items, Sergeant Waggit reached down and picked up the bracelet. With a quick motion from staring at the bracelet to swinging it down, Sergeant Waggit placed the bracelet onto his wrist and secured it to him so it would not come off. The bracelet had a strength built within it. There are some old Egyptian symbols on the side of the bracelet that's spelled out the message, "The one who wears this shall have the power to lift any boulder of any size." For a moment there Sergeant Waggit thought that the old relic that he had found was just a hoax, but then he realized it could be an advantage to him. He turned around and looked at that giant boulder that was sitting on the ground and decided to reach over and take a big grasp around it. He said to himself while picking it up, "There is no way that I'm going to lift this folder up over my head." Without a question the boulder was above his head. Sergeant Waggit could not believe that he just picked up a boulder that weighs over twelve hundred pounds. He then said to himself out loud, "This is awesome. I wish that I had this bracelet back in the day when I was in the military. It could bring me with the very most advantage to destroying or moving some really cool stuff, or even doing a funny gag or making a prank on somebody like moving their Humvee from one place to another without them even knowing it."

Sergeant Waggit noticed that the room veered to the right which could lead to another secret or back to where he was before where he had entered the cave. He followed the path around and discovered that it led to another open area but along where the water was flowing through it just like the open area was. Sergeant Waggit continued to follow the path of the water to see where it led him to. After walking for approximately five miles, Sergeant Waggit finally came to an end within the cave. There was a very large ball like an object near the end that glowed in the distance. With having much curiosity of the object, Sergeant Waggit decided to get a closer look as it could be something of value or it could be something that he could use. Once Sergeant Waggit reached the shiny object he noticed that it was a giant ball that looked like a clam's pearl. The ball was just sitting there all lonely with nothing around it just with some kind of a glow right in the middle. Sergeant Waggit reached out and placed his right hand onto the ball. The ground began to shake a little bit and the walls nearby zapped lightning bolts from them to the ball. Sergeant Waggit stepped back as he didn't want to be hit by a lightning bolt and wanted to observe what was going to happen. The giant like pearl flew up into the air and then started to begin to spin from a slow starting motion to a very fast motion in the clockwise direction. Then there was an outburst of energy that blew out against the walls causing debris to crumble down and allow the ground to tremble making a giant crack appear between Sergeant Waggit's legs. Quickly, Sergeant Waggit jumped out of the way and watched the ground physically rip open to a large channel underneath. Once the ground stopped moving, there was silence in the air and then the unspeakable happened within the cave. A giant tail reached out through the crack into the air. This tale was very large in size and had spikes on the end of it. Each spike was approximately twenty feet in diameter and about sixty feet long. The tell had to be at least three hundred feet in length with the endpoint being twelve feet in diameter and the starting point for what could be visible was at least forty eight feet in diameter. Then, a claw from one of the fingers of a monster's arm came out of the crack slamming onto the ground just in front of Sergeant Waggit. Another clock poked out along with the rest of his hand being tremendously in size came forth and slammed onto the ground just to the left of Sergeant Waggit. With a loud roar and a grumble growl near the end of the roar, out poked the head of a dragon-like creature. Once the head was completely visible and staring into the eyes of Sergeant Waggit, a secondary head popped out of the ground. Both of the heads were extremely large in size and had giant horns on the top of them. Both of the heads had very sharp long teeth and huge snouts for noses. The eyes were red and bloodshot full of demon spirit. The next were long and thick full of scales like fish that were in the underwater environment. The heads began to swing around slightly and spit up some kind of a fluid. Once the fluid came out one of the heads lifted its head up to the roof of the cave and shot a blast of fire trying to intimidate Sergeant Waggit. With this massive creature standing right in front of him, Sergeant Waggit had to think for a moment of exactly how he was going to destroy it.

Sergeant Waggit pulled out the double barrel shotgun and locked and loaded it. He began firing the weapon at the creature's mouth, nose, and eyes of each of the heads. It seemed like the creature was being shot as some flesh was coming off. As Sergeant Waggit continued to fire the double barrel shotgun at the creature's heads, the creature then began to spit fire towards him along with picking its arms up and slamming them down at his location. Sergeant Waggit did everything he could to dodge the fire and at him by running behind the large pillars that were holding up the ceiling. Then as the hands came down he dodged them by ducking and rolling past them. The creature would take its arm and slam it so hard on the ground that it would literally knock itself out for a little bit of time. Sergeant Waggit saw an opportunity to run up the creature's arm and face one of its heads real close. Using the double barrel shotgun, Sergeant Waggit was able to shoot the eyes directly in front, piercing more flesh off of them. The creature then threw Sergeant Waggit off and he landed on the ground in front of it. Sergeant Waggit got up and continued to fight against this creature as it wanted to kill him for everything.

He continued to dodge more fire outbursts and roll away from arms slamming down on the ground again. Once again, Sergeant Waggit ran up the arm to make another attempted attack against one of the heads of the creature. This time Sergeant Waggit emptied all of the bullets that he had for the double barrel shotgun into the head causing the head to fall to sleep or maybe die off. The other head of the creature knocked him down onto the ground once again. Sergeant Waggit ran around to dodge more fire outburst again and roll away from this of the creature's fist slamming down on the ground for a third time. Sergeant Waggit ran up the arm for the third time and took out his heavy cannon rifle. He began to unleash hell upon the second head and tell the head literally fell asleep or possibly dead. The creature knocked Sergeant Waggit back onto the ground in front of it and then climbed down into the depths of hell beneath the surface and disappeared without a trace.

Sergeant Waggit got up and jumped across the large crack in the surface. He headed down a main shaft that was through the cave and came to a very large area that looked like a dome like structure within the cave. The ground began to shake horrendously as once again debris fell from the walls and the ceiling tumbling onto the ground. Then, something opened up holes in the wall. There ended up being a total of eight holes that appeared in the walls which made two holes to the left, two holes to the right, two holes up in front, and two holes behind Sergeant Waggit. The holes were big enough to be like small little tunnels. Sergeant Waggit knew that something was going to happen as these holes did not just appear because of the ground shaking. The creature had returned from the underworld as it began toying with Sergeant Waggit. First, the creature poked one of its heads out of the front left hole. Another head poked out the front right side top hole. Both heads had come out simultaneously at different patterns but we're trying to attack Sergeant Waggit by biting at him and shooting fireballs directly towards him. Then within the other holes, the creature lungs its tail out trying to throw its spikes and sweep the area causing Sergeant Waggit to jump over the tail and duck underneath it as if it was high by the ground or low on the ground. Other holes within the walls exposed the creature's claws coming out trying to claw Sergeant Waggit. Each time the creature lunged apart out of a hole Sergeant Waggit had to dodge and hide from an attack. At the same time, Sergeant Waggit used his heavy cannon rifle to shoot directly at the creatures heads, claws, and tail. Sergeant Waggit saw that there were additional cases of rounds of ammunition for his cannon along with the double barrel shotgun. With a quick swoop in picking them up, Sergeant Waggit was able to secure the rounds of ammunition before he could be attacked by the creature. In return he was able to Lock and load his double barrel shotgun and began to unleash hell upon the creatures heads, claws, and tail. After a very long brutal attack and taking a lot of hits from the creature, Sergeant Waggit was able to expel the creature's breath until the creature could fall down. The creature then went into the walls and disappeared once again. Sergeant Waggit looked around the area just to make sure that it was safe from the creature or any additional attack that the creature could make.

Once the area was secured, Sergeant Waggit headed down one of the tunnels that was exposed through the walls in search of a way to get out of the cave. Along the way he had seen that there was a medical kit that would help him clear up the wounds that were slashed by the creature. Also, more ammunition packets were lying on the ground indicating that he was able to restock what he had expelled within the creature's carcass. Sergeant Waggit saw many different obstacles that he had to overcome along with having to fight off vampire bats and little tiny creatures that would lurk at him. After each small attack that Sergeant Waggit performed against creatures, small little ammunition packs and small health packs fell allowing him to replenish his depleted armor and weapons. Down a long hallway through the cave Sergeant Waggit saw daylight and knew that there may have been an escape to the outside parts of the cave. Running as fast as he could getting away from other small little creatures that were lurking behind him, Sergeant Waggit was able to reach the daylight that was just outside of the cave. As soon as he got outside of the cave Sergeant Waggit noticed that there was a staircase that he could climb up. step by step he followed the staircase all the way to the top which led him to a very large platform. Once standing on the platform in the middle area, the ground began to shake horrendously just like you did if he was inside the cave. In the distance within the cloudy mist Sergeant Waggit could see something flying but he couldn't make it out. As the object neared his location Sergeant Waggit began to notice what the object looked like. It was a very large creature, possibly the same one that he was fighting earlier as it had two heads, a very long tail, sharp razor claws, and two humongous wings that had a very large wingspan. Sergeant Waggit said to himself, "I cannot believe it. It is a two-headed dragon." The creature neared Sergeant Waggit's position and turned one of its heads towards him. With a loud screeching sound coming from its mouth and a very large spitting fluid, the creature began to shoot fire upon the grounds near where Sergeant Waggit was standing. He literally had to run and jump over the flames to keep himself from being burned. Then the creature flew off and flew around in the distance for another approach of an attack. This time Sergeant Waggit saw an opportunity to jump aboard this creature known as a two-headed dragon. As the creature approached his location, Sergeant Waggit leaped towards the large claws of the feet of the creature and saw that there were areas to grab a hold of. He began to climb up the claws and onto the feet. The creature would shake its foot as if it had an itch trying to make Sergeant Waggit fall off. However, with the power of the bracelet and the strength of his suit Sergeant Waggit was able to hold on as tightly as he could until the creature stopped moving its foot. Once the foot stops moving, Sergeant Waggit continues to climb up the foot until he reaches the leg that it was attached to. Sergeant Waggit looked up at the creature from his standpoint and was trying to figure out how he was going to destroy it. Within his vision Sergeant Waggit was able to see very large round glowing objects on the creature's body. These objects were the pressure points within each joint of the creature. Sergeant Waggit thought to himself, "If I were to punch or smash in each of those pressure points, then maybe the creature would fall to the ground to where I could obliterate it for good."

Sergeant Waggit headed up the creature's leg to its knee area where the first pressure point was. along the way he had to stomp what he was doing to hold on to the leg as the creature began to shake its leg trying to make him fall off. Once at the pressure point, Sergeant Waggit held on with one hand and began to punch as hard as he could, forcing the pressure point to go from a bluish color to a red color indicating that the pressure point was indeed attacked. Once the pressure point was changed in color Sergeant Waggit continued to claim the leg until he would reach the thigh, where the second pressure point is located at. Once again along the way Sergeant Waggit and to hold on for dear life as the creature tried to shake its leg in the event of trying to make him fall off. The power of the bracelet was so strong that Sergeant Waggit's grip would not let go. Once he had reached the second pressure point, Sergeant Waggit began to punch it as hard as he could until the pressure point turned from blue to red in color. The next pressure point was located in the rear of the creature halfway down the tail. Sergeant Waggit knew that if he was to head down that way this would be an interesting way of holding on as there's hardly anything to hold on to to begin with and the tail of course is going to whip. As Sergeant Waggit climbed off of the leg and femur into the creature's tail, the creature began to whip its tail up and down as far as it could trying to make Sergeant Waggit fall off. Of course the power of the bracelet would not allow him to fall but he did have a good swing to go with it. Once Sergeant Waggit reached the pressure point within the tail, he got a good grip and held on and began to punch the pressure point as hard as he could. The pressure point on the tail then went from a bluish color to a red color indicating that Sergeant Waggit has successfully altered the pressure point.

The next pressure point for Sergeant Waggit to conquer was located on the top of the back right in front of the tail. In order for Sergeant Waggit to perform this maneuver, he would have to climb all the way up the creature's tail and then somehow keep himself standing on the creature's back without falling off. Along the way of traveling from the tail to the back of the creature, Sergeant Waggit had to hold on as the creature began to swing the tail locked and right as hard as it could trying to force him off. Sergeant Waggit was able to get to the creature's thigh area to where he could climb up onto the creature's back. Along the way, Sergeant Waggit saw a harpoon weapon that was attached to the creature's thigh. After waiting for the creature to stop shaking itself so he doesn't fall off Sergeant Waggit reached out and grabbed the harpoon that was hanging from the creature's thigh. Once the harpoon was secure and attached to his utility belt Sergeant Waggit climbed up the creature's thigh and stood on top of its back just behind where the pressure point was. Sergeant Waggit then took out the harpoon and shot it directly into the back of the creature and attached the other end of the rope to his utility belt. With hopes that the harpoon stays within the creature's flesh, Sergeant Waggit began to punch as hard as he could on to the pressure point. While he was punching the pressure point, the creature began to shake horrendously back and forth trying to drop Sergeant Waggit. Of course even with having the harpoon attached to his utility belt and stuck into the creature's back, Sergeant Waggit swung around and in the air and all over but did not fall. Then he landed right next to where the pressure point was. Sergeant Waggit ran over to the pressure point and began continuing to punch it as hard as he could. After the second time of punching the pressure point, Sergeant Waggit was able to turn the pressure point from a bluish color to a red color indicating that he had successfully altered this pressure point within the creature's back.

The fifth pressure point was located on the side of the creature's ribs. Sergeant Waggit ran up the back of the creature as fast as he could and then got thrown down towards where the rib area was as the creatures slammed up against some rocky mountainside. The power of the bracelet allowed Sergeant Waggit to grab a hold of the scale that was attached to the creature's hive. He began to climb down the side of the creature until he reached the fifth pressure point that was right in the middle of the rib cage. While holding on for dear life, Sergeant Waggit began to punch the fifth pressure point as fast as he could and as hard as he could until it turned from a bluish color to red. After holding on for another shake of the creature trying to throw him off, Sergeant Waggit looked around and saw that the sixth pressure point was on the belly of the creature just underneath. Sergeant Waggit thought to himself, "That is going to be tough to reach as it is underneath the creature." Without a question, Sergeant Waggit started to climb down the rib cage of the creature using the power of the bracelet along with his harpoon to lunch himself over to the sixth pressure point that was located on the creature's belly. Sergeant Waggit carefully swung himself over to the belly of the creature where the sixth pressure point was just above him. Since he could not punch the pressure point as it was too far away, Sergeant Waggit took out his Rod of God and used it as an extension to punch the pressure point. While holding on very tightly with the power of the bracelet and the harpoon along with keeping the Rod of God in his hand, Sergeant Waggit continued to fight the creature's pressure point after the creature violently shook itself. The pressure point then changed colors from a bluish color to red indicating that the pressure point was now defective.

Now that six of the pressure points have been disabled, Sergeant Waggit had four more to go. The seventh pressure point was located on the right hand of the creature. Sergeant Waggit climbed across the belly of the creature using his bracelet and the harpoon. He reached the creature's right arm and began to climb down the arm. The creature began to shake the arm and swing it in multiple different directions trying to get Ser-

geant Waggit to fall off. But the power of the bracelet and a harpoon holding him on, Sergeant Waggit
was able to stay on the arm until the shaking
stopped. Then he continued to climb down until
he reached the creature's hand, which had razor
sharp claws and a very strong grip. Holding on to
the hand as tightly as he could, Sergeant Waggit
began punching the seventh pressure point elim-
inating the use of the right hand. While he was
punching the right hand, the creature tried turning its hand and grabbing Sergeant Waggit with its
very large claws. Sergeant Waggit dodged the attack of the claws that were upon his location. Once
the seventh pressure point was disabled, Sergeant
Waggit headed over to the left shoulder where the
eighth pressure point was located. Climbing
across both shoulders of the creature was not the
easiest and ideal thing to do as the creature kept
trying to do barrel rolls through the air trying to
fling off Sergeant Waggit. With the power of the
bracelet and the use of the harpoon Sergeant Waggit was able to get across both shoulders with very
short amounts of time. Then he attached his harpoon to the shoulder that had the eighth pressure
point. Sergeant Waggit then used the Rod of God
to apply a pounding pressure towards the pressure
point making it disabled. Once the pressure point
was disabled and no longer blue but in the state of
a red color, Sergeant Waggit saw that the ninth
pressure point was located on the neck of the right
head. He had to climb across the shoulders to

reach the neck of the right head. After using the power of the bracelet and the harpoon to reach the neck Sergeant Waggit was able to use the scales of the neck to climb up as if it was a wall. The left head was just swinging in the air and did not care the fact that Sergeant Waggit was on the other neck. Then the right eye of the left head turned and was able to spot the location of where Sergeant Waggit was hanging on to. The head then turned with a growling noise and lunged at Sergeant Waggit. While holding onto the rope of the harpoon Sergeant Waggit swung away from his current location to avoid being eaten by the left head of the creature. Sergeant Waggit returns to his location and begins to punch the pressure point to make it turn from a bluish color to a red color. During his attack, the left head returned, staring at Sergeant Waggit and then began to shoot fire in his direction. Without a question Sergeant Waggit cup to himself as close as he could to the neck on the opposite side of the blazing fire to prevent himself from being burned. Once the fire had extinguished itself against the right neck, Sergeant Waggit returned to the pressure point by swinging over with his harpoon. He then began to continue punching the pressure point until it turned to a red color. Once the pressure point was vanquished Sergeant Waggit looked around to see if there were any more pressure points that he needed to attack.

After looking around all over the creature

trying to discover if there's any more pressure points to be destroyed Sergeant Waggit was able to see a blue glowing round disc on the nose of the left head. He said to himself, "Son of a bitch. That is going to be a tricky one to destroy as I am not only going to be facing one mouth but two mouths that are wanting to do nothing but eat me." Sergeant Waggit then made his way across from one head to the other but this time was going to be a little different. He had to take his harpoon and put it into the creature's top of his nose. In order to pull off the most amazing stunt, Sergeant Waggit had to take out the Rod of God and wedge it between him and the nose. Once the rod was secured Sergeant Waggit took out his double barrel shotgun and began to unleash hell upon the last pressure point which was on the creature's left head nose. Of course, because the eyes of both heads are able to see Sergeant Waggit attacking the nose, both heads became vicious while trying to bite towards Sergeant Waggit. Then also the noses began to sniff in causing a huge draft of air blasting into the nasal cavities of both heads. The Rod of God was doing everything it could to keep Sergeant Waggit from being sucked into the nasal cavities, however, the help of the harpoon prevented him from going to the right head nose naval cavity. Along with all the terror that Sergeant Waggit had to dodge from the creature also had to shoot fireballs directly towards him not just from one head but both heads at the same time.

The tricky part was the head's not only shot the fireballs but also a stream of fire in a zigzag pattern from both heads. This put a huge burden on Sergeant Waggit's mind on trying to figure out how to get away from the blazing beams of fire. Sergeant Waggit thought of an idea as long as the creature did not sniff in he thought that he'd be okay. Sergeant Waggit removed the Rod of God and climbed as quickly as he could into the snout of the nose. The mouths breathed fire out as fast as they could trying to destroy Sergeant Waggit. As soon as the fire dissipated, Sergeant Waggit jumped out of the nasal cavity and reapplied the Rod of God to keep his distance away from the nose. The creature had no idea that he had climbed in its nose but it knew that he was not dead yet and so it continued to have mass attacks upon him.

After a long battle trying to change the color from blue to red on the nose, finally the battle came to an end as the pressure point upon the nose depleted into mercy and changed into the color red. The creature continued to fly though indicating that something else needed to be done to destroy it once and for all. All of a sudden there was a new blue mark that appeared between both necks among the chest of the creature. The Mark was in the shape of an x indicating that is the spot for the final attack. The only thing that Sergeant Waggit saw that all he needed to do was take the Rod of God and stab the area. He had no idea that just underneath that area was the heart of the creature. By stabbing through the heart will cause the creature to fall to its death. Sergeant Waggit worked his way over to the chest area just below both necks to where the heart was located. The creature knew what he was up to next and tried to lunge itself into the ground as hard as it could, making Sergeant Waggit lose his grip. However, with a harpoon in place and the rope attached to his belt, Sergeant Waggit was saved from an insane death and swung around for another approach upon destroying this creature. During the second time he took the Rod of God and shoved it right into the heart of the creature. The power of the Rod of God physically stopped the heart and sent a shockwave through the entire creature making it die in mid-air. The creature fell from the sky down into the ground, smashing itself deeply into the ruggish dirt creating a very large amount of debris.

Once the creature was on the ground and it took its last breath between both its heads, Sergeant Waggit removed the Rod of God from his heart and cleaned it off. He began to walk away from the creature but then out of nowhere the left head creeped open. As he turned around staring at the head indicating that the creature may do one last attack, Sergeant Waggit noticed something shiny that was stuck between two teeth. He ran over to the head and put the Rod of God in between the jaws to keep the head open. Using his knife from his harness to the side of him, Sergeant Waggit was able to pop out the shiny little gem that was stuck between the teeth. While holding the gem in his hand and feeling a burning sensation, he noticed that the gem was not a gem but instead it was one of his lost stones. Quickly, Sergeant Waggit reached into his pocket and pulled out the glove that's required to hold the stones. He slipped the glove on and then dropped the stone into the glove. With examining the stone closely, his computer system within his suit analyzed the stone to be the Secretion Stone. Sergeant Waggit took out the Rod of God and turned it sideways. He took out the stone and applied it to the rod. The stone latched onto the fourth notch that Sergeant Waggit cut out previously. The power of the Secretion Stone surged through the Rod of God with an electrical surge from one end of the rod to the other. The power upgrade gave Sergeant Waggit the ability to zap enemies and turn them into a puddle of red blood and guts with the absence of bones. Sergeant Waggit then secured the Rod of God and began heading down a path towards a very large tall standing Pyramid that looked very disturbing from the outside with all of its markings and presented a hellish vibe as there were two large salamander statues on both sides of the entrance.

CHAPTER FOUR

The Pyramid of Doom

Standing outside with a jaw dropping experience staring at a very unique pyramid, Sergeant Waggit noticed the really cool designs upon the stones and the two statues that had a devilish feel to them. The stones upon the pyramid had many designs on it and different types of symbols that represented different cults and other types of entities. Some of the strange symbols look like a skull with horns coming out of its head and a ring around its nose. Other symbols were symbols of snakes that were devouring a spirit indicating death was near or within the walls of this chamber. Other symbols upon the stones displayed eyes with tears coming off of them along with fingers being broken. The color of the stones were blood red with the lettering in black. The salamanders that were at the main entryway had many characteristics within their appearance. The left salamander had a body the shape of a human with a robe that was born similar to the Egyptians. Also this particular salamander had its mouth open with its tongue out indicating that it was breathing and searching for the lost souls. The salamander to the right was also wearing some kind of robe skirt that was from the Egyptian era and had a bow and arrow in its hands. The creature however did not have a human-like body but rather a top half that was salamander and the bottom half as a scorpion. The tail on the end of the scorpion body had a very large stinger indicating that this particular beast was very dangerous at the most. The mouth was not particularly open a lot but just enough to show two large fangs.

Sergeant Waggit walked up to the salamander statue that was on the right and began to steer it down as he was looking at all the details that were shown within the imagery projection of it. While looking at the statue, Sergeant Waggit began to hear a noise that was out of the ordinary as if it was the cracking of rock or debris falling. Then the top of the statue turned towards his location and began to pull the string back on the bow as if it was going to attack him. Sergeant Waggit took out the Rod of God and faced it towards the statue. He then activated the rod to prepare for an attack. The statue then turned back where it was and returned to its original state indicating that it was threatened by the Rod of God. Sergeant Waggit saw that the statue was afraid of the Rod of God. He then stored away the rod back to its holster within his back. Looking at the doorway and trying to understand who or what lives there was beyond anyone's dreams. Sergeant Waggit put his right hand onto his chin trying to determine what would lie within these walls as the doorway was so tall that even Optimus Prime, a transformer, could fit through it and jump if he wanted to without touching the roof. There were no doors at the entryway, just an open passage.

Once inside the pyramid Sergeant Waggit began to look around in search of anything that was out of the ordinary along with anything that could be dangerous to his presence. Within the walls lurking around inside the pyramid where these black creatures creeping down. Every time Sergeant Waggit would stop and look at the wall the creatures would stop moving and hide within the shadows around them. The ground was full of sand and rock debris from the residue of the pyramid being built. Within the first room that Sergeant Waggit was standing within there were lots of sarcophagus all over the place indicating that maybe this room was a burial room but not a burial room for someone important but rather an army or something within a city. In order to search for any other stones, Sergeant Waggit needed to open up every single sarcophagus and make sure that there was nothing within them except for bones. He began to open each sarcophagus one by one in the search for any other lost stones. One of the sarcophagus had ammunition sitting inside it for his double barrel shotgun. Another sarcophagus had other ammunition in there for his heavy cannon rifle. Then, Sergeant Waggit saw a crack in the wall that was nearby. He ran over to the wall and used the buttstock of his rifle that he was carrying and smashed the wall in exposing some kind of a doorway to another room. Within this second room there were two sarcophagus and an upside down cross in between them. The walls had blood that were dripping off of the sides and the sand was thick as there was blood mixed within. Sergeant Waggit walked up to each of the sarcophagus and opened them up. The one to the right had a medical pack that he could use along the way that would help him in case he got attacked. The one that was on the left had a map that he could use. The map disclosed the entire pyramid and every little area that was within it. However, some of the areas were very tricky to be able to reach as by looking at them on the map there was no doorway to them, not even a secret doorway.

As Sergeant Waggit left the secret area that he had discovered where he found his map to the pyramid, the shadows of the creatures that were climbing along the walls began to fall off the walls onto the ground. Sergeant Waggit heard a noise that sounded like footsteps but he couldn't see anything because it was dark and there was a little bit of light within the area but not enough to determine what was there. He took out the Rod of God and shot a round of plasma from it into the sky above the room which lit up the entire room like if you had a flare with it. The creatures that were lurking on the ground tried to stop but they were exposed to his viewing. Sergeant Waggit took out his heavy cannon rifle and began to shoot every single creature until not one of them was standing. While he shot each creature, Sergeant Waggit yelled out, "You bastards! You will die from trying to sneak up on my ass!" After all the creatures had fallen to their death upon the bullets coming from the heavy cannon rifle, Sergeant Waggit looked at the map that he had to determine the next location he needed to go. The room to the right was the next room that he had to explore and discover if there was anything that he needed along his path or if he could find another stone. Once entering the second room which was to the right of the first room, a door that was within the wall that was made of stone slides shut trapping Sergeant Waggit within the room. The ground began to shake a little as something was about to happen and then the walls moved a little exposing holes within each wall. With a random verse of shots, the holes within the walls began to shoot arrows into the room. Sergeant Waggit duck and dodged every single arrow that he thought he could get away from to keep himself from being shot at. After each wall had shot multiple rounds of arrows towards his location, the doorways that were shut opened up as they crumbled down to pieces allowing Sergeant Waggit to move on from that room. He felt something that was within the helmet that he had had no idea what it was and reached for it. Putting a firm grasp, Sergeant Waggit removed an arrow that had stuck into the side of his helmet but luckily it did not reach his flesh as it could have hurt him or even killed him.

The next room that Sergeant Waggit had to explore what's the broom to the north end of the room he was just currently in. According to the map, there was a table within the room indicating that it may have been a town hall of some sort. As Sergeant Waggit entered the next room he did indeed see the very large table which could hold up to sixteen personnel sitting around it. He, however, noticed that there were skeletons sitting at the table which drew to his attention that these people may have died sitting there or were all a hoax. At the far end of the table there was a button on and near the plate that was sitting there. Sergeant Waggit had a real high imaginational strength for enthusiasm and noticed that he had nothing to do but push that button. With ambitions to the high scale, Sergeant Waggit ran over to the other side of the table as fast as he could and slammed his face down onto the button. Not knowing whether it be a trap or something could dramatically happen to him after he pushed the button, Sergeant Waggit heard a screeching noise and then saw some dust fall from the ceiling. He looked up and noticed that the ceiling was beginning to crumble and out started pouring sand filling the room up. It looked all over the place trying to find an exit but the only exit that was nearby was clear across the room to the room that he originally came from. But then, Sergeant Waggit thought about it for a moment and decided that if the sand came from the ceiling, if the sand pours all down then maybe he should go up through the ceiling. Since he still had a harpoon, Sergeant Waggit used it to launch up into the ceiling latching on to something within another room that could have been above him. He climbed up the harpoons rope and reached the top where the sand was pouring out. After climbing through a bunch of sand that kept pouring down, Sergeant Waggit was able to latch on to something within the above room and he waited until all the sand stopped moving. Once the sand stopped moving, Sergeant Waggit took out the Rod of God and shot out some plasma into the sky once again into this room making it light up as if there was a flare in it. To his surprise, Sergeant Waggit saw a very unique statue that was right next to a door, a very large door. The statue was golden in color and had a bullhead similar to a sheep with horns that were very long and rounded into a spiral. The statue looks like a giant Minotaur that was also a creature myth of what the devil could have created himself. The statue of the creature was holding a very long stick and on the end of the stick had three chains hanging down with Morning Stars, large balls with spikes, attached to the end of them. The armor that the creature in the statue was wearing looked like some kind of a warrior outfit. The top half had some kind of vest with shoulder pads and latches that brought it all together. The bottom half was similar to some form of garment that would cover the genital area but had a belt that was 4 in thick in diameter and had a skull for belt buckle with flames coming out of its eyes. The feet of the creature were nothing but hoofs and the legs were demon-like structured.

The opening of the floor which was kind of like a doorway from the beneath chamber began to shut. Then, there was a very large clunking noise as longs appeared between the flooring making the room completely sealed trapping Sergeant Waggit within. The eyes of the creature that was in the statue began to glow with a yellow tint. Sergeant Waggit went up to the door to try to open it but discovered it was locked. He walked over to the statue and stared at the unique display design that it had. Sergeant Waggit looked at the statue and said, "You are some kind of royalty or some shit like that. I'm not afraid of you but I bet you're afraid of me... Huh bitch." The statue just continued to stay where it was, the eyes glowing yellow and the belt buckle eyes having fire coming out of them. Then the little demon that was on Sergeant Waggit's shoulder came out and decided to jump onto the statue. Sergeant Waggit yelled out, "Little Buddy, where the fuck are you going?" The little demon turned around and with a big smile on his face and grunted with putting his chin up. Then the unspeakable happened, as the eyes of the creature within the statue launched out some kind of strings or flesh in the form of strings towards the little demon. The strings wrapped around the little demon's body and then sucked it as fast as they could into the statue's eyes. This whole statue then began to glow and it started to move a little bit. Then the statue came to life and began to swing the Morning Stars around trying to hit Sergeant Waggit.

As he kept moving all around the room, Sergeant Waggit dodged the Morning Stars from coming in contact with his suit. He took out the double barrel shotgun and began to shoot at the moving statue. The bullets hit the statue causing little punctures within it but it didn't stop it for any purpose. So, he shouldered the double barrel shotgun and grabbed the heavy cannon rifle instead. Sergeant Waggit emptied an entire magazine full of rounds trying to destroy this creature and get his little buddy back but nothing worked as the bullets just kept bouncing off. He then harnessed the heavy cannon rifle and grabbed the Rod of God. First, Sergeant Waggit set out a burst of energy towards the statue to see what would happen. The energy hit the statue which caused it to stall out for a second but then it still didn't do anything to it. He's selected the second Stone that had the power to turn any living thing into a blob. With firing the rod with the power of the blob towards the statue, the statue began to glow red but still did not change shape or even disable it for that matter. Sergeant Waggit didn't think it'd be possible to engage both stones at the same time but discovered that if he was to bridge them it would cause a double jolt. The double jolt would create a giant plasma burst towards something and then explode like if it was a detonation of some sort. It took a while for both the stones to charge up but once they were charged the rod was ready to fire. Facing the rod directly towards the statue and only having one shot at it, Sergeant Waggit released a full burst of energy towards it hitting the center mass of the statue. The plazma burst out in the most impressive explosion lighting up the entire room to an extreme white bright light. Once the light went away, the statue was just standing there not doing anything and had a big hole through its belly area. The little demon climbed down through the statue and dropped down onto the bottom part of the opening within the belly. The statue then began to fall backwards as it was falling to the floor. The little demon jumped high into the air as fast as he could with as much strength as he could trying to get to Sergeant Waggit. With a quick reach and lunge towards the statue, Sergeant Waggit was able to catch the little demon within the grasp of his fingers at the absolute last second before landing on the ground. Once Sergeant Waggit was laying on the ground holding the little demon within the grasp of his hands, the little demon smiled and grunted and then ran up his arm to get back onto his shoulder. Sergeant Waggit stood up and walked around to see if the statue was going to get back up. The statue remained on the ground and the yellow eye tint and the fire within the belt's skull had gone out indicating that the power within the statue was no longer existent. The door that the statue guarded made a clunk sound allowing a lock to disengage within it. Sergeant Waggit walked over to the door and was able to push it open.

The door to the room that was next to the room that Sergeant Waggit was standing in opened up and exposed a whole nother room that was dark in color. there was a little light at the corner but not enough to light up the entire room. Sergeant Waggit noticed that there were torches that were hanging on the walls but they were not lit. He pointed the Rod of God towards the room and shouted out, "Let there be light!" A burst of energy blasted out of the rod and cast onto the torches enabling them to light up. The room lit up with enormous amounts of light exposing everything in sight for Sergeant Waggit to see. Within the room, there were cages that looked like they held animals of some sort. The animals were mutated creatures from the unknown and they kept making noises as they noticed there was light within the room. Sergeant Waggit kept his guard up as he walked into the room thinking there could be a surprise attack or maybe something will just come out and try to scare him. He walked through the entire room searching everything to see if he can find something he can use or if he could find a lost stone. On the wall to the left within the room, there were three doors and each one of them had a different marking upon them. The door to the right had the symbol of the devil relic and had the color of blood all over it. The door to the left had the left and right Moon crescents on it indicating that it could have been witchcraft and it was colored in blue like the oceans. The door right in the middle looked like a prison door that was black in color and had many slot openings that you could see through it and on the other side the door there was a small blaze like if a fire had broken out or something. Sergeant Waggit walked over to the doors and tried each door but discovered each one of them were locked. He tried using the Rod of God to apply energy to the doors to blow them open but however the doors were locked with some sort of spell.

Back in the middle of the room, Sergeant Waggit noticed that there was a type of puzzle that was on an incline. The puzzle was not necessarily easy to figure out but rather it was a sliding type where Sergeant Waggit would have to line up the pieces properly. Each of the pieces of the puzzle had slots within it as if something was to flow through it. Sergeant Waggit worked his magic with his hands and began to rearrange the puzzle pieces lining him up one by one. The puzzle was designed where you had to slide each piece around in order to make them lineup properly. After a short period of time and having lots of confusion, Sergeant Waggit was able to line up every little piece and make the puzzle complete. After the puzzle was completed there was a glow around it indicating that it had been completed. Then there was a jar that appeared above the puzzle. Sergeant Waggit reached out and grabbed the jar to look at it. He discovered that there was some form of red liquid inside it which could have been blood or possibly Mercury. Sergeant Waggit noticed that there was a saying in Greek right above the puzzle that said, "Pour here if you dare. But you must be aware. For things are hidden in plain sight. You have to be strong to win the next fight." Sergeant Waggit took the jar of fluid up to where the saying was and began pouring it into the drop slot that it had. The red glowing fluid went through the channels all the way through the entire puzzle. Once the fluid has reached the middle or the end of its travel within the puzzle, the right door and the left door are both unlocked but leaving the center door still locked. Sergeant Waggit took out a coin that he had within his pocket and flipped it in the air.

He called heads or tails and decided that heads would be the door on the right with the devil relic and tails would be the door on the left with the two crescent moons. When he removed his hand from his arm exposing the coin that was underneath it, to his surprise the coin was on the tails side facing up. Sergeant Waggit walked over to the left door that had the crescent moons on it and was able to open the door but just a turn of the knob. Through the door was a long hallway to a light just at the other end. Sergeant Waggit prepared himself with his weapons just in case something was to lurk out at him. At the end of the tunnel where the light was, Sergeant Waggit discovered that it was nothing more than just a flame on a wick upon the wall like if it was a giant candle. However, the candle had a block flame on it indicating that something had lit it up and exposed a form of witchcraft spells. On a table nearby there was a book that had an eye on it right in the middle. On the top of the book there was a devilish symbol and the saying, "I'll put a spell on you." Sergeant Waggit reached over and grabbed the book and placed it into his pouch. The light that was on the wall blew out indicating there is a huge draft that came within the walls of the tunnel all of a sudden. The door that he had originally entered in slam shut where he was now trapped. A type of which ghost appeared in the walls and lunged out some form of magic towards Sergeant Waggit trying to transform his suit into something other than human. Sergeant

Waggit took out the Rod of God and shot energy bursts directly at the ghost witches. The burst of energies that came out of the Rod of God did not have any effect on the ghost witches. Sergeant Waggit then yelled out, "What the fuck am I supposed to do now!!" Sergeant Waggit began to launch another energy burst at the go switches thinking that maybe a second time would cause them to be destroyed. Within his burst that came off the rod, the little demon that was his friend jumped off his shoulder and right into the burst of energy. The little demon then began to transform into a large demon which then began attacking the ghost witches. The demon ripped the ghost witches to pieces until they were no longer visible. Sergeant Waggit said to the little demon which was now a large demon, "Alright my little buddy, now let's turn around and shrink back down your size and hop on my shoulder." The little demon which was now a large demon did not respond to him whatsoever and completely had ignored his request. Sergeant Waggit then said again, "Come on my little buddy, turn around, shrink down, and get on my shoulder so we can move on." The little demon which was now the large demon turned around and was not a demon at all. The creature had a body of a demon yes but it had the head of one of the ghost witches. Sergeant Waggit began to shoot lots of energy burst towards the head of the demon trying to get the ghost witch off of it. After multiple rounds that were spent with the

Rod of God, finally the ghost witch flew off and disappeared into sight. The demon then shrunk down to his normal little tiny size and ran over to Sergeant Waggit. He reached down and picked it up and watched the little demon climb back onto his shoulder.

After the little demon was on Sergeant Waggit's shoulder, the door that was shut and locked from the entryway to the hallway that he was standing in had unlocked and reopened. Sergeant Waggit walked down the hallway until he exited the door. He then walked over to the other door that had the devilish relic on it and opened it. Through the door was another hallway heading all the way down to some form of another door that had fired all the way around it. Sergeant Waggit walked all the way up to the door and then tried opening the door but noticed it was locked. He thought about it for a moment to figure out how to unlock the door but then notice that there was some bluish-type glow that was around the fire and thought out loud, "I Wonder if this fire is not really a fire at all and if it's a spell that has cursed this door." Sergeant Waggit reached in his pouch and took out the spell book that he had retrieved from the other room. He flipped through the book until he found a page that had a picture just like the door with fire. There was a spell cast upon it and if the spell was said in reverse then it would reverse the effects and allow the fire to go away. However, there was one consequence that would occur when this happened. If the spell was broken by someone who is not a virgin the individual would have to face their worst fears. Sergeant Waggit said out loud, "I would have to face my worst fears... Oh Dear God! No, no I will not... I must, not!" Sergeant Waggit's biggest fear was himself becoming more dark than the devil himself. He knew that he had a dark side to him and knew that if it got out of hand it would take over his life and make him do things that he didn't want to do. When he was in war a lot of the dark side of him came out. Sergeant Waggit refused to face his worst nightmare of all. Then again, he is in the worst place you can imagine and he's about to break a spell that's going to make him face his worst nightmare.

Sergeant Waggit looked at the words in the spell book and began to recite them. At first the words are written in the normal direction as they were written in the book. Then the words were written backwards in the book as for the reverse spell. After Sergeant Waggit read the first spell to himself quietly he had reached the second spell which is the reversal of it. He then began to say the spell out loud. Sergeant Waggit began reading, "Enter shall you and, within air the up pick, apart torn are men, strong are we together, fire of wisdom and strength, brutality all to immortal, door this upon." The spell had been broken and the fire upon the door perished and there was a clunk noise to the doors locking mechanism. Sergeant Waggit reached out and grabbed the door's handle and turned it which allowed it to open. He walked through the door and as soon as he got on the other side which was in some form of a room the door slammed shut behind him trapping him in the room. On the other side of the room a light appeared that was extremely bright. Due to the brightness, Sergeant Waggit used his right arm to cover his eyes so he would not be blinded. Then the light had a shadow cast upon it as if something was stepping through it. The light then disappeared and standing right in front of Sergeant Waggit across the room was himself but in a more evil dark presence. The dark presence within his opposite was holding the same weapons as he had. The only difference between Sergeant Waggit and the dark presence of himself was he was good rather than evil at most times. Both Sergeant Waggit and his evil self had a little demon on their shoulders. Sergeant Waggit thought about it for a moment and wanted to see which demon would be stronger. He knew that his demon could be a lot stronger than the dark side as it knows his true identity. the dark side of him standing across the room is a mirror image of just his evil within but not his entire spirit.

And so the conquest began as the evil side of Sergeant Waggit across the room started charging him as fast as he could. Standing there with no fear to be applied as he knew that the dark side was just a mere image Sergeant Waggit reached out and took out his double barrel shotgun. He began to shoot multiple rounds at the dark side of him that was lunging directly at him. The rounds were hitting the armor and piercing it causing pieces of it to fly off and eventually flesh to come out. However, there was one consequence to this matter of attacking his other self. Every time a bullet would hit the armor or hit the flesh, Sergeant Waggit would feel the same within his own body but notice that there was nothing wrong with his armor or his flesh, just pain. Sergeant Waggit continued to fight the dark side of him until all its armor was gone. After dispensing all rounds of ammunition from his double barrel shotgun and heavy cannon, Sergeant Waggit was left to use the Rod of God. The powers within the rod were very strong but not strong enough to destroy this evil within his evil self. The little demons that were on their shoulders climb down and begin attacking each other. it was quite the sight to see as the little tiny little creatures were fighting each other on the ground. The evil side to Sergeant Waggit's self began to grow enormously large. It threw an uppercut hitting the little demon through the air and towards Sergeant Waggit. As Sergeant Waggit yelled out in terror as the little demon was flying towards his face, the little demon landed directly onto his mouth. Before Sergeant Waggit did anything the little demon climbed down his throat and got inside his body. Having a weird feeling within, a transformation began as Sergeant Waggit turned into a massive demon-like creature but also looked like a cyborg at the same time. With the strength of the little demon inside him and the power of the Rod of God, Sergeant Waggit was able to attack his evil dark side and make him lose all of his powers. Once the evil side of Sergeant Waggit had been conquered by the power of the Rod of God and the little demon inside Sergeant Waggit, it fell to its knees and bowed with honor of defeat. Sergeant Waggit watched his evil side bow and kneel down to the ground holding the rod in both hands just like if it was holding a sword. Then the evil side to him disappeared and vanished into a fiery dust leaving a glow within a floating fireball. Sergeant Waggit walked across the room and over to the glowing fireball that was floating at arms reach. He reached out and grabbed the floating fireball. With a great observation while staring at the glowing fireball, Sergeant Waggit saw something within its center core. Sergeant Waggit tried to remove the core from this floating fireball but could not figure out how to open it as it was secured with either magic or some type of relic. A door to the side of the room opened up. Sergeant Waggit carried the floating fireball and walked through the door as it could lead him somewhere either good or bad. As he passed the door, Sergeant Waggit looked around and saw that he was in some kind of a chamber that had multiple different types of spells all over the place. Almost all of the objects within the chamber that had spells on them. There were sarcophagus, chests, and bones that were scattered all over the room. The bones were broken down as they were soldiers of a very long time ago that had been slaves within Tartarus. Sergeant Waggit took out his spell book and began to read off different spells trying to unlock everything that had a spell cast upon them. One by one each object broke the spell and revealed what was inside. Sergeant Waggit found rounds of ammunition for his double barrel shotgun along with rounds of ammunition for his heavy cannon. After searching the entire room and unlocking every single structure by breaking their spells, Sergeant Waggit was confused as he found everything he needed but he still could not figure out how to open up the floating fireball. Then out of nowhere, a wall began to move and another sarcophagus came sliding out of the wall. Sergeant Waggit walked over to the sarcophagus and slid the cover across exposing what was inside. Inside the sarcophagus there was a lever and a text in ancient Hebrew that said, "Pull me to reveal the secret." Sergeant Waggit reached out and grabbed the lever. He pulled the lever back locking it into a position. Once the lever had moved all the way back to a locked position, a clunk noise sounded within the sarcophagus and a little door opened up along the side of the sarcophagus. Within the door there was a little chamber that had the same shape and structure of the floating fireball. Sergeant Waggit took the floating fireball and put it into the little chamber within the sarcophagus. The door to the little chamber had ancient Hebrew written on it as well. The words spelled out, "Close this door and lock the top to the sarcophagus and you shall reveal the power to melt ice and burn holes within any lair." Sergeant Waggit shut the door with the floating fireball inside the chamber behind the door. The sarcophagus began to glow red and shook all around. Then the glowing effect and the shaking went away. Sergeant Waggit removed the lid to the sarcophagus and saw a glowing item that was sitting right in the middle. He noticed that it was a stone of some type and didn't want to burn himself again, so he reached into his pocket and pulled out the glove that would prevent any Stone from burning his flesh. After putting on the glove, Sergeant Waggit reached into the sarcophagus and picked up the stone. He had no idea what the stone was or what it was even for as he could not remember what it was when he had originally found it. The stone was red in color and in the middle of it it had some kind of flowing lava. Sergeant Waggit thought about it for a moment then he remembered what the stone was known as. He had picked up the magma stone. Sergeant Waggit placed the stone into the next slot within the Rod of God. The rod began to shake and reveal a red outline around it. The tip of the rod changed shape to reveal a small type of tube that could dispense something. Once the Rod of God stopped shaking and became normal again, Sergeant Waggit tested the rod against one of the walls that was nearby. An amazing thing happened as the rod dumped magma all over the wall causing the wall to melt to nothing. Since there was no other opening within the chamber, Sergeant Waggit walked through the wall that he had melted and was able to exit the pyramid.

Once he was outside the Pyramid of Doom, Sergeant Waggit followed a path that led him to a beach that had multiple entry points to a sea. He looked over and saw that there was nothing in sight except for objects to check to see if there was anything he needed. He continued searching around the beach for anything he could use and discovered a boat that was tied up at a dock. Sergeant Waggit looked around to see if anything or anybody was watching him and saw nothing so he boarded the boat. With a flick of a rope off the dock and steering the rudder towards the open Sea, Sergeant Waggit had no idea what he was in for. The boat led him through an unknown sea to an open area where there were multiple rocks sticking out of the ground and a huge fog bank that covered up part of the sea. Sergeant Waggit used the rutter to dodge all the large rocks that were sticking out of the sea. He thought that being in this sea was peaceful and not full of danger, however, a danger within the sea awaits before him.

CHAPTER FIVE

The Forbidden Sea

As Sergeant Waggit continued his journey across the sea that he was floating on within a boat, he continued to dodge all of the giant rocks and kept the boat afloat as it hit many large waves that kept coming at him. The waves then became calm and up ahead was a huge bank of fog. Sergeant Waggit grasped the rutter with a really strong grip showing some kind of fear that lurked within him as the fog was coming closer to the ship. As the boat floated into the fog, Sergeant Waggit awaited for anything that could surprise him with an attack. As the boat was surrounded by nothing but fog and keeping Sergeant Waggit blindness to the world around him, the boat hit something and stopped. The boat began to shake a little bit as if something was standing or attached on the bow. Sergeant Waggit took out his heavy cannon rifle and was ready for anything that was about to come near him. As the fog began to clear up a little bit around the boat Sergeant Waggit got a glimpse of what was standing on the bow. With claws on the feet and huge wings that had a wingspan of over fifteen feet, stood a demon gargoyle. Without hesitation Sergeant Waggit shot his heavy cannon rifle and the creature, knocking it off the boat. Then the boat cleared the fog bank and showed the reality within a new realm. Within the sky there were thousands of demon gargles flying everywhere. As the boat continued through the sea, each demon gargoyle flew down and tried to attack the boat, ripping pieces of the wood off trying to sink it. Sergeant Waggit knew that his weapons were not going to be any good for this with the exception of the Rod of God. He harnessed his heavy cannon rifle and took out the Rod of God. With the new power that he had discovered from the tomb Sergeant Waggit was able to launch balls of magna towards each demon gargoyle causing them to burn up in the sky and plunge into the sea. After a long firefight, Sergeant Waggit whipped the sweat off him and said to himself, "Glad that shit is over." Then the boat came in contact with a very large rock which caused it to stop in the sea. A very large demon gargoyle with a wingspan of fifty feet splashed out of the waters on the other side of the rock up into the air. The large demon gargoyle began to shoot fire towards the boat making the wood catch fire. Sergeant Waggit used all of his power that he could within the rod and his weapons to destroy this evil gargoyle. However, it was too late for him as the boat began to sink into the sea. Sergeant Waggit grabbed everything he needed and jumped off the boat at the very last second and grabbed onto the nearby rock that the boat was attached to. Sergeant Waggit turned around and watched the boat sink below the surface of the sea. He turned around after watching the boat sink and saw the evil gargoyle plunge into the sea.

There were lots of rocks all over the area within the sea. Sergeant Waggit looked at all the rocks to determine how he was going to explore each one as he is trapped in the middle of the sea where he can't go anywhere. The rocks were spread out like a lily pond configuration. Some rocks were tall and jagged where other rocks were flat and had cave-like structures within them. Sergeant Waggit found a very large stick on the first rock he was standing on. He picked it up and looked at it and said to himself, "I can use this stick to travel between each rock." With a firm grasp onto the stick, Sergeant Waggit plunged it into the sea and used the stick to pole vault to another rock. Sergeant Waggit safer you landed himself onto the next rock. The rock that he had landed on was jagged in shape and had some sort of cave within it. Sergeant Waggit used the Rod of God to light up the path as he began walking through the cave within the rock. inside the cave there were many types of bones all over the place indicating the death has been here. Above his head was a whole bunch of sharp pointy rocks that were attached to the roof of the cave. Sergeant Waggit looked up at the sharp pointy rocks and said to himself, "I hope that those fuck'n rocks don't come falling down on me." As Sergeant Waggit continued walking through the cave searching for anything that he needed to find if there was anything, the ground began to shake a bit as if there was some kind of earthquake happening. The rocks above his head shaked and shattered against each other making a clanging noise. Sergeant Waggit covered his head up with his arms and kneel down as he sheltered himself thinking that those sharp pointy rocks were going to fall. Then the earthquake had stopped and the shaking and clanging noises within the sharp pointy rocks came to a halt.

Sergeant Waggit stood up very slowly and looked up to see if any of the sharp pointy rocks were going to fall but it seemed like all of them were secured and not going anywhere. He then continued his path through the cave and walked around to find anything that he needed. Sergeant Waggit found a whole bunch of crates that were within the cave scattered all over the place. He began to use his rod to open each one at a time trying to discover if anything was inside them. One of the crates he opened had all the ammunition he needed for every single weapon he had. On the other hand, the other crates had creatures of vampire bats lurking inside them. As each lid was pried off, Sergeant Waggit had to shield his face as vampire bats wormed past him with a great rush from flying out of the crates. Once all of the crates were all open Sergeant Waggit began heading back to the entrance to the cave. As he was just underneath the sharp pointy rocks, an earthquake began to happen again. This time Sergeant Waggit was not so lucky as the sharp pointy rocks started breaking off and falling down breaking on the ground near him. He began to run as fast as he could to reach the exterior entranceway of the cave. At the very last second with only inches to spare Sergeant Waggit jumped out of the cave and onto the platform of the giant rock he was on. All of the rocks within the cave crumbled causing the cave to collapse to where there was no more of an entry point. Sergeant Waggit looked at the rubble that was falling down in front of the cave and said, "Well, I am sure glad that I made it out."

Sergeant Waggit retrieved his long stick and pole vaulted to another rock. When he landed on the next rock, the form of the rock was flat with a small plane wreckage. Sergeant Waggit hurried over to the plane as quickly as he could to see if anything was salvageable within it and if he could repair it to get off this seabank area. The plane was unable to be repaired as all the engines were separated from the wings and the body was broken into several pieces along with wiring being shredded due to rodents chewing on them. As Sergeant Waggit entered the cabin area of the plane he noticed that all the seats had nothing but skeletons in them indicating that the people died on the plane and decomposed into bones. He began searching all around the plane for anything that he could use. As Sergeant Waggit passed one of the passengers that was nothing but bones, the bones began to move a little bit. Sergeant Waggit turned around and went over to the bones and stared at it. He took out his Rod of God and used it to move the bones around but found nothing around it. the little demon that was on his shoulder grunted and then stared at the bones as if he saw something within them. Sergeant Waggit then turned back around and continued his search for anything within the cabin as if maybe something just kind of jolted the bones and it wouldn't worry him. While he was searching the plane, the skeleton that was sitting in the seat that moved a little had a seatbelt around its waist. The skeleton took its left arm and unbuckled the seatbelt and then quickly returned its arm to the resting position that it was originally in. Sergeant Waggit heard a noise that sounded like a strap was zipping fast across something and turned around quickly to see what happened. He walked up to all the skeletons and was looking at every one of them and noticed that one of them did not have a seat belt on. Sergeant Waggit said to himself, "What the fuck. I know that all of these fuck'n skeletons had seatbelts on when I came in here... I believe I remember." To be sure Sergeant Waggit grabbed the seatbelt that was not attached to the skeleton and secured it so that he knew that all of the skeletons had a seatbelt around them. He turned around again to continue his search and hoped that nothing else was going to surprise him. Then all of a sudden, all of the seat belts detached themselves from all the skeletons. There was nothing but a bunch of loud sipping noises with a click noise coming from each one of the skeletons. Sergeant Waggit turned around very quickly as he heard the noise and saw that there was no movement whatsoever. He quickly ran over to the skeleton to see what it was but saw that all the skeletons were still sitting in the same place that they originally were, however, none of them had a seat belt on. This really worried Sergeant Waggit as either there is something within the plane that was causing this to happen or he's about to have an episode of something terrible.

Sergeant Waggit turned around again but this time it didn't go anywhere he wanted to make sure that it was safe before he continued his mission. After a few moments of standing there in silence Sergeant Waggit turned around very quickly to see if anything had changed. With his jaw dropping all the way down the floor indicating that he was shocked and afraid, Sergeant Waggit saw every skeleton standing in front of the chair staring directly at him. As he reached for his double barrel shotgun, the skeletons began to climb over the seats and rush him as fast as they could. With shooting round after round Sergeant Waggit began to destroy each skeleton until they fell down to pieces. After all the skeletons have been destroyed to nothing but pieces, Sergeant Waggit took out the Rod of God and pushed the bones around to ensure that they were not going to make any sudden surprises. Sergeant Waggit found rounds of ammunition within the plane and was able to restock his double barrel shotgun. As Sergeant Waggit exited the plane the ground began to shake horrendously that he was standing on causing him to fall onto the ground onto his knees. He tried turning around towards the plane and as he was staring at the plane he noticed something. The bones were collecting to each other and creating a massive skeleton. The skeleton's arms picked up the engines and began turning the blades. the skeleton legs punch through the base of the body of the plane and lift the plane high into the sky. The middle of the plane broke open as a huge head came sticking out with glowing red eyes. The skeleton roared as loud as it could with a blast of air rushing past Sergeant Waggit's face. Sergeant Waggit knew that this creature looked like some form of a titan and it could have what he needed.

The giant skeleton swung each arm at a time trying to hit Sergeant Waggit with the rotating blades from the engines. Sergeant Waggit dodged each blow as fast as he could. The skeleton then began to throw parts of the plane towards him.

Sergeant Waggit had to use his weapons to destroy each part in front of him so they wouldn't hit him causing his armor to be pierced. Then for a moment the skeleton would act like it was stuck and couldn't move. Sergeant Waggit noticed when the skeleton would stop moving at a yelled out, "No it's my fuck'n chance!!" Sergeant Waggit ran over to the skeleton as fast as he could and used the power of the Rod of God to disintegrate each part of the skeleton with blasting magma at it. He could only reach the feet at the time so as long as he melted the feet away then it would shorten the skeleton's height. The skeleton continued to fight, throwing its arms at him trying to hit Sergeant Waggit with the spinning blades that were attached to the engines and then again trying to throw parts of the plane at Sergeant Waggit. After dodging the engines and destroying the parts that were flying at him, Sergeant Waggit ran over to the skeleton once again as it was stuck and not moving. Sergeant Waggit dumped even more magma onto the legs now causing the skeleton to become even shorter in height. The skeleton was now down to where it had no more legs and it was sitting on its waist on the ground. At this point the skeleton knew that it had to do a different counterattack against Sergeant Waggit. It's one of the arms around trying to hit him with the blades but then it detects the blades causing them to zip across in front of Sergeant Waggit. As those blades zipped in front of his location, Sergeant Waggit dodged them the best that he could without being in contact with them. Then the skeleton titan began throwing larger chunks of the airplane parts trying to destroy Sergeant Waggit's armor. Since the parts were much larger in size, Sergeant Waggit had to use the Rod of God and destroy each part with burst powers. Then the skeleton got stuck again and Sergeant Waggit ran over to it as quickly as he could and began to melt the rest of the skeleton from the head down as he could reach it. He kept pouring more magma all over the skeletons until there was nothing but a puddle. After the skeleton and the plane were no longer existent, a little blue glowing ball appeared floating just above the puddle of magma. As the magma hardened Sergeant Waggit walked across it to grab the floating ball. He noticed that there was something inside it that looked like a stone and said to himself, "Ha, I found another stone." Sergeant Waggit was able to open the small blue ball and take out the stone. He noticed that something was wrong as the stone did not burn his hand. He said to himself while staring at the stone, "If this is not a stone, then what the fuck is it?" Sergeant Waggit knew that he may need this fake stone as it may be a key to something.

Sergeant Waggit secured the fake stone into his bag. He then continued his mission pole vaulting between each rock in the surge for either the real stone or something else that may actually help him. After pole vaulting passed at least twenty different types of rocks, Sergeant Waggit came across another cave within a rock. With lots of care, he entered the cave with caution to make sure there were absolutely no surprises that were going to happen this time. As Sergeant Waggit walked through the cave, he noticed something strange about it. The walls had some kind of secretion on them and looked like a giant skeleton as they were like ribs on the walls. He thought to himself, "Either I'm in a cave or a dead whale." As he continued his adventure through the cave, Sergeant Waggit stepped into some kind of goo that was on the ground. The goo was sticky and prevented him from moving fast at all; in fact it made him move extremely slow. While he was trying to get out of the goo, Sergeant Waggit heard a loud roar that came from deep inside the cave. Down the cave was some kind of light that looked like a fire. Sergeant Waggit noticed that the light was coming towards him. Then as he was still stuck in the sticky goo, the fiery light appeared right in front of him. Sergeant Waggit looked at the light and noticed that it was not just a fire but a floating demon's head that was burning on flames. He took out his double barrel shotgun and began unloading rounds of the ammunition into the floating demon burning head. The head exploded shooting fire all over the place then dispensing the flames into the goo. With the sound of the double barrel shotgun echoing through the cave, more floating demon heads that were burning on flames came flying as quickly as they could through the cave. Sergeant Waggit did everything that he could to destroy all of the heads that were flying towards him. When all of the demon heads that were on fire were all destroyed, a larger demon head that had a glowing effect to it came out. Sergeant Waggit shot at it with everything that he had to destroy that head. Once the head blew up within the cave, the fireballs that were cast about the explosion caused multiple little explosions. Behind Sergeant Waggit's location was one of the explosions occurring causing rubble to fall closing off the entryway to the cave. Sergeant Waggit turned around and slowly went up to the rubble. He slammed his fist into it trying to break it but nothing happened. He then yelled out, "Fuuuck!! Now what?!!" Sergeant Waggit then spared his breath and turned back around to find a way out of the cave.

After traveling through the sticky goo for a long time within the case, Sergeant Waggit was able to get out of the sticky goo and begin heading down the cave to find some form of exit. Then the ground began to shake again as another earthquake hit. Just beneath Sergeant Waggit's feet the ground opened up exposing a hole in the ground. Sergeant Waggit fell through the hole and then landed on the rock as it was like a slide with water. He slid all the way around zipping around

trying to stay within the sliding rock and not falling off of it as parts of the slide were exposed to
molten rock underneath. As he was sliding down
the rock with water rushing around him, Sergeant
Waggit so light at the end. The light came closer
to his viewpoint as he kept on sliding down the
slide. Then as the light became extremely close,
Sergeant Waggit was able to stand up and get ready
to jump out. With the count of three and the light
was right there Sergeant Waggit jumped as he said
three. He landed on another flat rock that was outside of the cave. Sergeant Waggit looked around
and noticed that he was not close to the original
location that he was at and did not have his pole
to pole vault either. Sergeant Waggit said to himself, "Damn, without my pole, I cannot go over to
anymore rocks." The ground began to shake again
as another earthquake was occurring. All of the
rocks that were within the vicinity of the area were
crushed into the sea leaving just the rock that Sergeant Waggit was standing on to be the only one
visible for miles.

Sergeant Waggit saw that the water right in
front of the rock within the sea began to swirl. The
swirling effect became so big that it caused a giant
whirlpool to appear. Then the whirlpool disappeared and there was dead silence among the sea.
Sergeant Waggit took out the fake stone from his
bag and tossed it into the sea. He then said to himself, "Well, that was a waste and I no longer need

this fake stone." Right after the fake stone plunged into the sea, the water in the sea right in front of Sergeant Waggit's location began to bulge up through the sea as if there was air underneath it. Sergeant Waggit leaned over to see what could possibly be underneath the water. Then all of a sudden, a giant demon gargoyle with a wingspan of five-thousand feet and stood as tall as a skyscraper building came blasting out of the sea. The giant demon gargoyle opened its mouth and let out a loud roar towards Sergeant Waggit causing him to fall onto the ground shielding his hand across his face. Sergeant Waggit got up and began to fight this creature. He emptied every magazine he had for his heavy cannon rifle and expelled every round within his double barrel shotgun. Then Sergeant Waggit used the power of the Rod of God to propel massive attacks against this huge creature. The giant demon gargoyle would scream causing the ground to shake horrendously and also flap its wings towards Sergeant Waggit causing him to fall onto the ground. Sergeant Waggit would get back up and continue fighting this creature. After a long firefight with the giant demon gargoyle, the demon became angry and charged Sergeant Waggit. It tried to use the very large clause that it had on its feet to grab his armor. Sergeant Waggit would dump magma from the Rod of God all over the giant demon gargoyle's feet. The demon was immune to the magma, however, when the magma would harden, the magma would hold the giant demon gargoyle for moving. Sergeant Waggit saw an opportunity to run up the gargoyle feet, climb up to its head and use the Rod of God against it to poke out its eyeballs. After both eyes were destroyed and putting magma all over the head of the gargoyle, the creature knocked Sergeant Waggit down, making him fall onto the rock that was within the sea. The giant demon gargoyle then plunged into the sea perishing forever.

Upon the rock that Sergeant Waggit was standing on, a crate appeared. Sergeant Waggit walked over to the crate and used the rod to tear off the top. Inside the crate was a new weapon that he could use. Inside the crate laid a missile launcher that had markings on it that he had never seen before. Sergeant Waggit had no idea where the missile launcher was crafted or who crafted it. Sergeant Waggit reached into the crate and secured the newly found missile launcher. He shouldered the missile launcher with the strap attached to it and turned around as he heard something come from the sea on the other side of the rock. Sergeant Waggit walked over to the other side of the rock to see what the noise was and noticed some sort of portal. He looked at the portal and said to himself, "Well, what could be more depressing... stranded at sea or falling into a portal which I have no fuck'n idea where the fuck it is going to take me." Sergeant Waggit thought about it for a moment and then jumped into the portal. The portal transported him to an unknown land that had no sea, however, there was nothing but a hot dry desert.

CHAPTER SIX

The Poseidon Desert

Standing in the midst of a strange desert with sweat pouring down his face, Sergeant Waggit looked around to see if there were any signs of life or refuge. He began to walk about the land to find refuge and food as his rations were getting low on his journey. Along his way through the desert, Sergeant Waggit saw holes in the ground. Each hole was a venting path for steam and would also create geysers that would propel water to an astonishing height of fifty feet. Sergeant Waggit did everything he could to keep away from the geysers as they looked dangerous. In order to walk through the desert, Sergeant Waggit had to jump over the geysers and hope that he would not get hit by any of them. Some of the geysers did not let off steam but instead, there were demon-like spiders that would climb out of them. Sergeant Waggit saw spiders climb out of the nearby geyser hole and began to head in his direction. Sergeant Waggit took out his double barrel shotgun and began shooting all of the spiders. The demon spiders looked just like a giant camel spider but with a demon head and had the colors of black and red like a black widow. The spiders had huge fangs dripping with enough toxins to kill an elephant in one bite. The spiders would jump through the air trying to attack Sergeant Waggit similar to a face hugger in the movie "Aliens". The spiders looked similar to a face hugger, however, they did not have a tail. The spiders were very vicious and took about two to three hits from a double barrel shotgun to kill them. Sergeant Waggit spent most of his rounds of ammunition trying to protect himself from the killer spiders. Then, Sergeant Waggit tripped on a termite mound exposing what was inside it. After a bunch of termites left the mound, a box of rounds for his shotgun appeared. Sergeant Waggit picked up the rounds and reloaded his shotgun for the next attack.

Sergeant Waggit continued his journey across the sandy hot desert looking for refuge and food along with any type of stone that may be hidden. Sergeant Waggit saw a mountain top within the desert and ran to the top of it so he could get a better glance of his surroundings. When arriving at the top of the mountain top, Sergeant Waggit stopped and took out a pair of binoculars and began to search the land of the desert for any refuge. With little to no luck, Sergeant Waggit found nothing within his vision around the desert. Then the unspeakable happened as Sergeant Waggit had no idea that he was standing on a sinkhole. The sand that was below his feet collapsed sinking him deep into the abyss. With little knowledge of the desert, Sergeant Waggit fell through the sand into a Kingdom that was underneath the desert. As he was looking around the newly found Kingdom, Sergeant Waggit noticed that there were statues holding tridents as they were guarding something. Sergeant Waggit thought to himself and with his past he remembered that the only place that could have tridents was the lost city of Atlantis. He knew then he could be at the lost city Atlantis or it could be just a mirage or some kind of a replica design of it that's in the underworlds of Tartarus. Sergeant Waggit scouted the newly found Kingdom for any items that he could use along the way and for any stones that could be found. Within the thick walls of the Kingdom under the sand there were many different channels leading in different directions. Each channel could lead Sergeant Waggit to finding valuable items like health and food or it could also lead to something that would resemble a trap. Sergeant Waggit must choose wisely and use the computer system within his suit to analyze each channel for any sudden death traps. Sergeant Waggit activated his computer system so he would be able to be notified of any strange structures. Along with his computer system, Sergeant Waggit also took out the tracking device and began to track any motion that was within the channels as he may not be alone. The cute little demon that was sitting on his shoulder started making some grunting sounds as it knew that there could be dangers lurking by. Sergeant Waggit reached over and patted his little demon that was on the shoulder and said, "Don't worry little guy, it'll be alright." The little demon smiled with a gleam on his face and grunted with joy as an expression.

Sergeant Waggit began to head down the nearest pathway that was within a chamber in surge for valuable items that he needed. Along his way he found multiple different holes in the ground. The holes are similar to the ones that he saw up on top of the desert that let out a bunch of spiders. Sergeant Waggit heard a noise that was sounding like some type of clicking object and stopped as the motion detector picked up some form of movement. At that moment, little demon type spiders come crawling out of the holes hitting directly towards his location. Sergeant Waggit quickly took out his double barrel shotgun and began to eliminate all of the spiders. Once all the spiders were vanquished from sight the little demon on his shoulder began to clamp and smiled with a grunt in cheer. Sergeant Waggit looked at the little demon and said, "I know little guy, we got them." Sergeant Waggit looked at the motion detector and saw that it was silent once again. Then it began to continue his search within the chamber that he was walking through. at the end of the chamber there was a crack in the wall that looked like there was something else on the other side.

Sergeant Waggit grabbed the Rod of God and used it to strike the wall with the power of one of the stones. With the power of destruction, the crack in the wall crumbled down exposing what was on the other side. After climbing through the hole that was exposed, Sergeant Waggit discovered a secret chamber within a chamber. Inside this chamber there were three tridents being held up by statues. Each trident was a different shape and could resemble going into some form of mechanical device. Sergeant Waggit used the strength of his suit to remove the tridents from the statue's grip. After securing all three tridents and attaching them to his cargo strap on the back of his suit, Sergeant Waggit headed out of the secret chamber into the regular chamber down the hall and all the way down to the main lobby area where he originally discovered all the chambers. Inside the lobby area there was a mechanical device that looked like a giant clock with gears applied to it. Within the mechanical device there was a specific pattern that looked like one of the tridents. Sergeant Waggit removed the trident that he would think would fit inside that pattern and without a question put the trident directly into the pattern on the mechanical device. At first nothing happened and the device did not turn, rotate, or move in any form of way. Sergeant Waggit felt discouraged as he thought that the mechanical device was damaged but then he remembered that the lost city of Atlantis was originally covered in water. Sergeant Waggit removed a flask that was supposed to be full water and discovered that there was not even a drop left in it. He said to himself, "I'm probably a million miles away from Earth and have no fuck'n water whatsoever." Sergeant Waggit's next objective was to find some water within the chambers that he lurks through.

Sergeant Waggit settled up and began to head down another chamber that may have water within it. He won't for hours and did not find any source of water whatsoever, however, he did find something else. Within the chamber that he was walking through, Sergeant Waggit noticed a particular item that was laying on the floor. The item was a plant of some sort which Sergeant Waggit knew that he could harvest water from the leaves from it. He picked up the plant and stored it into his pouch. Sergeant Waggit then continued his search through the chamber to see if he can find anything else that's very useful on his mission. He continued to walk but then discovered that the chamber ended up all the way back to where he started. With frustration in his mind, Sergeant Waggit began to think that this place is nothing but a huge maze and could lead him to madness. While using his computer system to analyze each chamber, Sergeant Waggit discovered one of the chambers that may just be what he's looking for as there was a brilliant shine within it. He began to run down that chamber in search of that brilliant shine indicating that it could be a stone. Once he arrived at the brilliant shine within the chamber, Sergeant Waggit discovered that it was not a stone but however another mechanical device. This mechanical device was similar to the first one that he saw but I used different markings and had a different key structure. Sergeant Waggit took out the other two tridents and looked at them. It looked at the keyhole that was within the mechanical device and looked back at the tridents and noticed that neither one of them matched. Sergeant Waggit thought to himself, "Well, there must be another key or trident somewhere around this area." He then marched his area on the computer system within his suit and continued walking through the chamber. With some great luck, Sergeant Waggit saw that there was a crack among the ceiling. He took the rod of God out and smashed it into the ceiling where the crack was allowing the rocks to crumble down. Sergeant Waggit then used a rope that was within his pouch to throw up with a grappling hook and latch onto something within some chamber or something like that above the chamber that he was in. He climbed at the rope and entered into another secret chamber. This time, this secret chamber had a sarcophagus within it along with a trident that was standing next to it. Sergeant Waggit tried to remove the trident but had no luck. Then he decided to remove the lid to the sarcophagus which led to some kind of trap that was made from salt.

The power of the Rod of God applied a shield around him protecting him from the blast of the salt. As he looked inside the sarcophagus, underneath the pile of bones was another trident that was broken but yet still useful. Sergeant Waggit removed the trident from the sarcophagus and secured it on the back of his suit. He headed out of the secret chamber and back into the other chamber that he was in and ran down the hall to find that same mechanical device that he was at before. Once arriving at the mechanical device, Sergeant Waggit removed the newly found trident and stuck it inside the key slot as it fit perfectly. Once again absolutely nothing happened as they trident just sent inside the key slot of the mechanical device. Sergeant Waggit talked to himself while staring at the mechanical device, "I wonder if all of these devices are connected somehow."

Sergeant Waggit quickly headed back down through the chamber to the main section where all the chambers aligned. He checked off his list of the chambers that he went through using the computer system within his suit. Sergeant Waggit discovered that there were two more chambers to head through. He began to head down one of the chambers in the surge for something that would be useful to him. Within the chamber there was another mechanical device that had a key slot and to his luck one of the tritons that he was carrying was booked identical to the key slot. Sergeant

Waggit removed the trident from his back and placed it into the key slot hoping that it would do something. Once again, absolutely nothing happened as the trident just sat there. Sergeant Waggit tried to remove the trident from the key but however the trident was stuck. So, Sergeant Waggit left the trident inside the key slot within the mechanical device and began to head back to the main area where all the chambers connected. Once he was in the main area, Sergeant Waggit headed down the last chamber that could possibly help him find what he's looking for. While he was in the chamber the ground began to shake horrendously as if an earthquake began slipping tectonic plates underneath the ground. The ground cracked open in front of him leaving a distance to be able to make a jump that was greater than what he could do. All of a sudden a giant arm from a Titan popped out of the crack and slammed into the ground. Sergeant Waggit decided to take a risk and run across the arm as quickly as he could before the arm would do anything. Right when he was at the edge of the elbow of the arm that was sticking out of the crack within the ground, Sergeant Waggit made a jump for it to catch the edge of the other side of the crack. He barely made it to the other side with holding a grappling hook in his left hand and hanging by the edge of the crack. The little cute demon on his shoulder climbed off onto the ground, turned into a giant beast, and helped drag Sergeant Waggit up onto the land.

Then the little demon, which at the moment was a giant beast, transformed back down to its little cute size and ran back up Sergeant Waggit's suit so it could get back on his shoulder. Sergeant Waggit looked at the little cute demon that was on his shoulder and said, "Thanks little buddy." The cute little demon grunted and smiled as he was pleased to help his master.

Sergeant Waggit ran through the chamber and came across another mechanical device. He took out the last trident and looked at it and said to himself, "I hope that this trident that I am caring is the correct one that will fit this device as I don't see any other areas that could house anything like this anymore within these underground chambers." With casting it directly into the mechanical device, the trident fit perfectly securing it in place. Of course after the trident was secured nothing happened within the mechanical device. Sergeant Waggit looked at the device and tried to rotate the trident but could not budge it for any means whatsoever. He then began to head back to the main lobby area where all the chambers connect together. Once Sergeant Waggit was standing in the middle of the main lobby area, he took out the plant that was within his pouch and placed it on a table that was nearby. Using the Rod of God, Sergeant Waggit was able to harness the power to excrete one drop of water from a leaf upon the plant. As the drop of water was secured by the power within the Rod of God, Sergeant Waggit walked over to the mechanical device that was in the middle of the room and let the drop of water fall onto the trident.

The drop of water hit the trident and a miracle happened right in front of Sergeant Waggit. All of the tridents were old and looked like a stone statue, however, when the drop of water touched the trident, the trident mechanical device transformed into a golden structure that was beautiful and brilliant to look at. Sergeant Waggit could not believe his eyes in front of him but then again he couldn't believe anything as he's in Tartarus within the middle of the unknown universe. Sergeant Waggit knew that the space time continuum could be completely different than what is within the Earth. After the mechanical device and the trident were both golden in structure, Sergeant Waggit heard a clunk noise coming from each of the chambers where he had walked through. Then right in front of him the Trident that was attached to the mechanical device turned and clunked downward into the gears making the gears move. As the gears were making a clunking noise that was sounding like a clock, the ceiling opened up allowing a giant trident to fall down with chains attached to it as it was coming down slowly. Once the very large trident was in the grasping distance of Sergeant Waggit's reach, Sergeant Waggit took his hands and grabbed the trident. The trident was so heavy that it smashed down under the ground breaking it into a million pieces. Once the trident was no longer in Sergeant Waggit's hands a glowing object appeared right in the middle of the mechanical device. Sergeant Waggit walked over to the mechanical device and got a closer look at what the glowing object was. He discovered another stone that was hidden within the land of the desert. Sergeant Waggit reached in his pouch and took out the glove that he had and put it on. He reached out and grabbed the stone and analyzed it with his computer system. The system stated that the stone was the Black Diamond Stone. Sergeant Waggit took the stone and secured it into the Rod of God which allowed it to change another color and give it even more power. The new power that the Rod of God has would take any Jewel that is on the ground and break it into pieces so that you could retrieve anything that was within it, even if the jewels were indestructible. Sergeant Waggit thought that that was the only thing that he had come for and had no idea what was about to happen next.

A secret passageway had opened up within the main chamber area allowing Sergeant Waggit to continue his quest through the vast desert. Sergeant Waggit secured everything that he had and decided to walk through the passageway. After walking through a really long tunnel that let him to light that indicated he was going outside,

Sergeant Waggit discovered that he had entered a boneyard for the deceased Titans. there were Titans all over the place as if there was a huge battle that occurred a very long time ago. There were helmets that were applied on the ground, arms and legs scattered all over the place, and the belly beasts of every single Titan stacked on top of each other as if they brutally beat each other to death. Sergeant Waggit walked about through the Titan boneyard trying to find his way through to the next era of him discovering his other lost stones. Along the way he found multiple objects that would help him like health, armor, and ammunition. After climbing all over the boneyard Titans, Sergeant Waggit came across a valley where there were no Titans. He stomped and turned around as the ground began to shake. While looking at the boneyard he noticed that the Titans were moving and he could not believe his eyes. Piece by piece the Titans stacked together to create one giant Titan with six arms, four legs, and two heads. This newly created giant Titan stood as tall as ten-thousand feet in the air. Sergeant Waggit stood there and stared at the Titan in fear as he had no idea how he was going to destroy this large beast. The Titan grabbed multiple other body parts of other Titans that were still on the ground and began to chuck them at Sergeant Waggit. Using the Rod of God, Sergeant Waggit used the power to slingshot the items that were coming directly at him to fly back and hit the giant Titan. As each body part

hit the Titan they would damage the Titan making and scream in terror. Then the Titan would
slam it down onto the ground on its hands and
knees and run as quickly as it could up to Sergeant
Waggit. Then the mouths on both heads would
try to bite Sergeant Waggit. It was not easy to get
around the Titan as the ground kept shaking horrendously making Sergeant Waggit fall down. He
dodged every blow that the Titan threw at him,
whether it was body parts of other Titans or trying
to bite him with the mouths of the two heads on
the Titan.

Once the Titan got tired it would slam onto
the ground allowing a passageway for Sergeant
Waggit to climb up and attack the main joints that
it had. Sergeant Waggit only had a short period of
time to make such attacks before the Titan would
stand back up. After multiple attacks applied to
the joints within the Titan, finally a defeat allowed
the Titan to fall to the ground, smashing and destroying all parts of the body to just being broken
up once again. Sergeant Waggit went through the
rebel of all the body parts of the Titan to see if
anything was left behind. After searching for a
very long time, Sergeant Waggit was about to just
give up; he noticed a glowing substance within a
foot of the Titan. He quickly ran over to the foot
to get a closer look. To his eyes, Sergeant Waggit
discovered another stone that was floating above
the toenail of the giant Titans foot. He took out

the glove once again from his pouch and secured the stone. Using his computer system within his suit, Sergeant Waggit was able to analyze what the stone was. The computer system acknowledged that the stone was known as the Sierra Blood Stone. When attaching the newly found stone to the Rod of God, the rod then changed color once again and gave it a new power. This time the power was strong enough to make anything that was dead and bring it back to life but follow the lead of the person who bears the rod in their arms. This new power would allow Sergeant Waggit to create an army that could follow him and attack anything that he needed. For what was going to happen next, this power may just come in handy.

CHAPTER SEVEN

Land of the Forgotten

The Titan has fallen to the grounds of the desert within the lands of Poseidon. Sergeant Waggit searched the remaining fragments of the Titan for any items that will help him on his journey. On his way out from the Poseidon Desert, Sergeant Waggit noticed a portal that was open. With curiosity, he jumped into the portal hoping that it would not lead him to his death. The portal sent Sergeant Waggit to another destination within the known universe. After exiting the portal, Sergeant Waggit looked around to see where he was. He thought that he may still be within the unknown lands of Tartarus as it is very vast across the known universe. To his vision, Sergeant Waggit noticed a very large pyramid within a strange land that was covered with rubbish as if it was a wasteland. He advanced towards the pyramid with his heavy cannon at the ready in case there were any surprises that could lurk out at him. Once arriving at the entryway of the pyramid, Sergeant Waggit noticed some artifacts that were displayed above the door hinges on a plaque. He reached over to his left arm and activated the scanner which in turn sent a beam upon the artifacts. The computer within Sergeant Waggit's suit analyzed the symbols from the artifacts which displayed a message. The message said, "Beware of what lies within the walls of this tomb. One wrong step and you will wake the unknown." Sergeant Waggit thought about what the message said with a puzzle look on his face. Then he said to himself, "Well, I will just have to watch my six and ensure that I do not wake whatever is lurking inside the walls of this pyramid." Sergeant Waggit then began heading into the pyramid with great caution. He pushed the door open as they were both shut and walked inside the main entryway. Once Sergeant Waggit was standing inside the pyramid, the doors slammed shut behind him as if there was a draft or a ghost pushing it. Quickly he turned around to see if anything was there and discovered that there was nothing. A chill went down his spine as he knew that he was not alone and it is a good possibility that something was going to jump out at him.

Sergeant Waggit walked through the main lobby of the pyramid which had glamorous effects within it that resembled some type of Golden Palace. The artifacts within the pyramid were beautiful and remarkable designs. He walked over to one of the unique design artifacts that was very beautiful in design and picked it up. While looking at the beautiful artifact, Sergeant Waggit said to him-self, "My, what an extraordinary piece of work. This is so beautiful I've never seen anything like it before." He put the piece of work back down onto the table that it was a pawn and continued his journey through the main lobby. Along the way as Sergeant Waggit was walking he kept hearing some kind of strange noise that was coming from behind him, as if he was being followed. Sergeant Waggit quickly turned around with a flash to see absolutely nothing that was behind him with the exception of the artifact that he saw earlier was now on a table that was nearby. He said to himself, "What the fuck. Was that artifact on that table or this table, I can't remember." Sergeant Waggit turned around and began to walk through the lobby some more and he started here in the noise again. This time he turned around very quickly as fast as he could and noticed that the artifact was now lying on the ground behind him. Sergeant Waggit pointed his rifle directly towards the arti-fact as he knew something was not right. After some time of staring at the artifact with a rifle pointed directly at it, Sergeant Waggit decided that nothing was going to happen so he lowered his guard and let the weapon point away from the arti-fact. Then all of a sudden the artifact stood up all by itself as if someone was standing there and lifted it. Then without a question, the artifact flew off the ground and hit it directly at Sergeant Wag-git trying to hit him in the head. he lifted his rifle directly towards it and unleashed hell upon the artifact until there was absolutely nothing remaining but pieces scattered all over the lobby. While staring at the pieces that were scattered all over the place like if they were guts blasted after a grenade hit someone, Sergeant Waggit witnessed the metal melting down to a blob and then gathering to each other to form a new artifact out of gold. The new artifact Rose from the ground but instead of being a beautiful piece of work that looked glamorous and gold color now had a gold texture in the form of a goblin. The goblin rushed at Sergeant Waggit with its mouth wide open and teeth showing as if it was going to attack him. Quickly, Sergeant Waggit harnessed his heavy cannon rifle and took out the Rod of God. Using the power from the rod that can melt anything, Sergeant Waggit cast in a pond the artifact that was now a goblin and forced it to become a blob once again. Even though the blob was trying to form again in some other design, the ground at that point melted and allowed the blob forming to fall beneath the pyramid. certain when I get chuckling and laughter said to himself as he was looking at the blob when it fell, "Ha ha, you little fucker. That is what you get." Sergeant Waggit then turned around and continued his journey through this unique beautiful pyramid in search of something that's going to help in the longest way. As he entered the next chamber that was around the corner from where he was, Sergeant Waggit noticed a really large chessboard that was very cool in size. He said to himself out loud, "Can it be. I mean... it looks like I'm in a chess game similar to a movie that I watched that was known as, "Harry Potter and the Sorcerer's Stone".

A large light appeared lighting up the entire chessboard. There was a piece that was missing on the white side of the board. Sergeant Waggit walked over to the side that was missing and looked at all the pieces to determine what piece he would be if he was to stand there. Sergeant Waggit noticed that he would be a queen next to the king. He decided to step into the square where the queen would stand. All of the sudden all the doors within the room slam shut hard and locked. On the black side of the chessboard, a pawn moved forward two spaces. Sergeant Waggit didn't know how to make the pieces work correctly so maybe he thought he could just go up to the piece and push it. He left his space and walked over to a pawn that was in the front row. Sergeant Waggit put all his Force within the suit to push the piece on the chessboard but nothing happened. Then he returned to his place and looked at where the pawn was. He saw that there were numbers on the board and decided to call out the numbers as if it was like a battleship game. Sergeant Waggit yelled out, "B Six!" The pawn on the right in the front row moved two spaces forward from B Four to B Six. Sergeant Waggit then said to himself, "Okay, I got this shit.

King, you are going to fuck down." The black side of the chest board moved another pawn forward exposing a bishop to move. Sergeant Waggit could not bear to allow the bishop to take anyone out so he made a night move forward and called out, "Knight to D Seven." The White Knight mood up and then over to the location that was yelled out. The black side then took the bishop out and stomped in line with the White Knight. Sergeant Waggit then set out loud, "You son of a bitch, you are not going to beat my ass." Sergeant Waggit saw an opportunity to take his other night and block the bishop with a pawn right behind the knight. Of course the black side used the bishop to take out his white knight. Sergeant Waggit then forced the pawn to take out the bishop. The black side of the board then decided to allow a black knight to come out and fight. Sergeant Waggit it's on opportunity to take out another pond and make it where it was right in line to destroy the night. The black side of the board thought it would be interesting now that the queen is available to wander upon the board. With a single move the queen moved all the way over into an angle to where the square that the white king was standing on. A loud voice yelled out in the background, "Check!" Sergeant Waggit looked around and saw that the king could not move in any place whatsoever, so in order to block the queen it was either he moved or he moved a pawn forward. The most wise decision was to allow a pawn to move forward. The black side of the board moved his queen across and destroyed the pawn exposing another check against the white king. The only other move that he thought would be good was to move forward himself and protect the king as he is a queen on the board but he didn't want to be stabbed to death like the other characters were being destroyed. Sergeant Waggit had a different idea and noticed that the distance between the king and the rook was open. He then said to the king how loud, "King, I command you to change places with the rook." The rook began to move towards the king and then the king got up and moved on the other side of the rook. The black side of the board did not like that move whatsoever and chose to move out another pawn instead. Sergeant Waggit decided to allow another night to advance towards the black side of the board. Of course the black side of the board was not too enthused by his decision and advanced another pawn to try to take out the night. However, Sergeant Waggit had better plans with his teammates that he's playing with as he knows chess very well and his computer system can analyze who's going to be that winner of the outcome.

The black side of the chessboard moved its other Bishop into place trying to get the check that it wanted. With not having any luck of making the check into place, Sergeant Waggit advanced his night forward and put the black king into check. Where his night was it would benefit his fight as he knew that when he was going to make the other king move he could take out the rook. The black side the board king had to move one position to the right. Sergeant Waggit then allowed his night to fight and destroy the rook onto the right side of the board. The black side of the board then advanced the other night trying to eliminate his king similar to the way he was doing it because it uses a mathematical equation for every move that is made. Sergeant Waggit's computer system stated that he moved the right side bishop and put the king into check. of course computer systems are only as smart as the people who built them and even though the probability of the computer system being correct could have a high or low chance, Sergeant Waggit decided to turn off the system temporarily just so he can use his gut as he knew what was going to happen was going to cause another loss of another piece that he's going to lose that's very valuable. After turning off the system temporarily, Sergeant Waggit advanced another pawn forward to take out other pawns. After a very long discreet play that was causing death to many pieces within the chessboard, there were only four pieces left on the black side and three pieces left on the white side. Both sides still had their kings, queens and one knight each. The black side, however, had a rook they could still use. Sergeant Waggit put it to the fourth effort of destroying the rook. Using the knight, Sergeant Waggit made the black sides rook fight to the death leaving the white knight standing in the rooks place. The black side of the chessboard then forced the queen upon the king's location for a chance to get a checkmate. Sergeant Waggit had to step forward to block the queen from making such a move. Since the white night was kiddy cornered to his location, Sergeant Waggit was safe from the black side's queen for now. Sergeant Waggit then yelled out, "I'm going to finish you off now you son of a bitch!" As the black knight was stuck near a corner trying to move and allowing its black queen to try to take out the white queen, Sergeant Waggit portraying to be the white queen ran across the board as fast as he could in a diagonal fashion and stood right next to the king. Where he was standing his white night was also positioned to that square as well. The Black Knight that was holding a very large sword then dropped the sword to the ground and crumbled to pieces as it was destroyed. The voice came on real loud in the background and said, "Checkmate! You have victoriously won against the black side of the chessboard. Congratulations." Once the speaker was done talking, all of the doors unlocked and revealed the new passageway outside of the chess game area.

Sergeant Waggit nodded and looked at the pieces and said to them, "I'm sure glad that you were on my side or I would just not know what to fuck'n do." The piece that he was looking at nodded in agreement to his provocative mind. Sergeant Waggit then headed out of the room into another room that had a bunch of mirrors within it. He looked around and then set out loud, "What the fuck. Is this another test?" again the doors slam shut behind him locking in place and a laughter began to appear among the mirrors. Sergeant Waggit yelled out real loud, "That's Enough!!!" He then took out his heavy cannon rifle and began to shoot every single mirror until they were all destroyed. Once all the mirrors were smashed to nothing but pieces the doors unlocked and the noise of the laughter went away. Sergeant Waggit then said, "Now that's how you fuck'n do it." With a cleared check point within the room, Sergeant Waggit continued walking through into the next room which had beautiful sarcophagus all over the place. Each sarcophagus was made of pure gold just like King Tut's but had more gold and more valuable items upon them. He said to himself as he was rubbing his hand all over one of the gold toppings, "Who or what is inside these sarcophagus that deserve to have so much gold." Sergeant Waggit decided to take upon himself and use the Rod of God to open the top to one of the sarcophagus. Using all of his power, Sergeant Waggit was able to open the sarcophagus exposing a demon structure body inside it. Sergeant Waggit didn't think it was a grilling big idea about the demon-like structure being alive as it was clearly dead for a very long time. However, Sergeant Waggit has a funny and twisted side to him to keep himself motivated within his journey. He decided to pick up one of the arms that was to the demon like structure and make it look like it was waving to him. Of course just like any bones that were brittle and frey, the arm detached from the body. Sergeant Waggit noticed that the arm had detached and decided to place it next to the body back inside the sarcophagus. He then picked up the lid and put it back on so the body would not be disturbed whatsoever. Once finished in that room looking for anything that could benefit his time through his voyage, Sergeant Waggit moved on into the next room which then the doors slammed shut behind him. He looked around the room and saw that it was just empty and there was nothing there. Then all of a sudden, the door behind him burst open and all of the creatures that he had seen that were considered to be dead or skeletons that were within the pyramid came bursting through the door. All of the skeleton creatures ran past them as quickly as possible and started to climb on top of each other inside the middle of the room. Once as many as one-hundred skeletons were all packed together into a giant ball, the doors slammed shut and locked. Sergeant Waggit dodged the ball as it began rolling around the room trying to destroy anything in sight along with dropping a few of the demon-like skeletons onto the ground and fighting him. Using every weapon possibly known to shoot at every single skeleton, Sergeant Waggit scattered the bones all over the room as if it was like a puzzle being torn apart. To his acknowledgement, Sergeant Waggit could not understand the reason why the bones kept reflecting back to each other and making these skeletons come back to life as if they were zombies. Then he thought about it for a moment and took out the Rod of God. Sergeant Waggit said to himself, "Well, if you can't beat them then make them join you." He saw one of the skeletons run from him. Sergeant Waggit ran after the skeleton and yelled out, "Come back hear you son of a bitch! All I want to do is play a game with you!" The skeleton zombie-like creature kept on the run until it turned around and faced Sergeant Waggit. With a flick of the rod and a powerful dispersal coming out the end, Sergeant Waggit turned the zombie-like creature into an ally army member. He then commanded the zombie-like creature to attack the other zombies. After fighting multiple zombie-like creatures and turning all of them into an ally army member, Sergeant Waggit had the entire crew of zombie-like creatures on his side. However, there was something or someone that wanted to challenge his ability to keep the creatures by his side. A creature by the name, "Swarm", came out of one of the sarcophagus that was from the other room and came into the room floating through the wall. Sergeant Waggit saw this new creature as it was similar to the creature named, "Shaft", but instead of being black it was white. Sergeant Waggit said to the creature, "So, who are you and state your business?" The creature responded by saying, "My name is Swarm. I am here to stop you from creating such armies to your side. I am Shaft's evil sister and will stop at nothing until I get what I want, which is revenge." Sergeant Waggit took out his rocket launcher and tried to shoot a rocket at this new creature but for some reason it had some kind of spell upon it preventing any damage. The creature cast a spell upon the zombie-like creatures and made them come at Sergeant Waggit. Reaching inside his pouch along his waist, Sergeant Waggit pulled out the spell book that he had kept from the other tomb that he was in. Quickly he found a spell that could possibly help him in this sticky situation. Sergeant Waggit read the spell out loud by saying, "Bones from coffins to goo, be strong and bust a move." The zombie-like creatures stopped in their tracks and stood there staring at Sergeant Waggit. Performing similar to a break dancer, Sergeant Waggit began to dance in front of the creatures. The creatures then began to dance following each step that Sergeant Waggit was doing. Sergeant Waggit continued to dance forcing the creatures to follow his footsteps for every move he performed keeping them occupied. Swarn then yelled out, "NO! This cannot be! Ugh!" Swarn created a huge bubble around all of the creatures that were dancing and transported them back into their sarcophagus where they will remain for eternity. Then she escaped flowing through the room into the unknown. Sergeant Waggit noticed that there was something glowing on the ground where the creatures were dancing. He walked over there and saw that it was another stone. Sergeant Waggit reached into his pouch and took out his special glove. He slipped it onto his hand and secured the stone that was on the ground. After turning his computer system back on, Sergeant Waggit allowed the system to analyze the stone so he would know what he just retrieved. The system acknowledged that the stone was known as the Mortality Stone. Sergeant Waggit took this new stone and applied it to one of the slots that were available that he carved into the Rod of God. When the stone snapped into place within the rod, the color changed again but this time it was glowing blue and green combined. The new power that the rod now can cast out was known as green acid. The acid was so powerful that anything that would get in its way it would burn it to oblivion. The answer was strong like molecular acid which can melt metal. Sergeant Waggit said to himself, "This is cool. I now have the power to spit acid on people." The Rod of God now has more functions than ever that will allow Sergeant Waggit to advance his weaponry power to defeat most astonishing creatures.

As Sergeant Waggit was leaving the tomb that he was within, he noticed that the ground had a big crack upon it which he was so afraid that it could give out. Sergeant Waggit walked fairly slowly across the crack so he would get to the other side as it could be the exit of where he needed to go. But then all of a sudden, the crack broke open and he fell and plunged to an unknown land, netherworld. Inside the chamber that he had gone to within the depths of the netherworld there were many unique caverns and tunnels that Sergeant Waggit will have to explore in order to find a way out. Netherworld was a similar world to Tartarus that was run by Hades but was known for the dungeons of his torturous depth. To survive in this new land, Sergeant Waggit will have to face three different heads.

CHAPTER EIGHT

The Chains of Cerberus

The Netherworld is a place that Sergeant Waggit will never forget. The Netherworld was full of cities in ruins being destroyed with mass destruction and fire in all directions along with washed up banked ships that were broken as they collided with multiple rocks within seas around the universe. The people within the lands of the Netherworld were nothing more than demons and gargoyles that served Hades for a purpose. Lakes and fire upon the top of the lakes were treacherous in fueling the enormous heat, which is not really felt in person but kind of like being by a volcano where you see the lava as it has cooled off and you're able to walk on top of it but yet it is extremely hot underneath. The air had a smell that would bring your senses to life as carcasses that were rotting nearby along with the vicious drool of the monster's creature laid upon the lands and the seas. Thick clouds were hovering above the seas shadowing anything that goes through it casting them into darkness of all eternity. A pathway around the seas led all the way to a gate where a dungeon kept the secrets of the Netherworld.

Sergeant Waggit began heading down a narrow path that was heading all the way up towards the dungeon in the far end of the Netherworld. Along the way he encountered a broken ship that was across the path. The ship looked black with black sails similar to the Black Pearl. However, on the front of the ship there was a young woman carved in wood with a beautiful dress that had multiple different flowers upon it. The flowers bloomed with a combination of wonderful tulips and roses. The most mysterious thing of all within the carved woman was the necklace that she was wearing. The necklace had a black chain that went around her neck along with a cross that was upside down and a pentacle around it signifying that she was Hades's bride. Hades did have a bride and her name was Freyja. The curved woman upon the ship was a signature piece of work handcrafted by Hades himself to resemble the loss of his bride, Freyja. The meaning for Hades bride's name was nothing more traditional than saying she was beautiful, loving, and full of death. However, death could not even keep her alive as she betrayed Hades and tried to overthrow his throne to rule the underworld along with Shaft. Since then Hades would not forgive her unworthy workmanship upon his throne and cast her into the seas where all the dead lie. She strung herself up to a ship but unfortunately that wasn't strong enough as the creatures of the sea ate her body into pieces leaving her to do nothing but be part of the sea. To get back at Hades, Freyja climbed aboard a ship and drove it straight into his belly with full darkness to overthrow his kingdom one more time. The father of Hades, Lucifer, cast upon a barrier between the two that were battling within the Sea of the Dead. By doing so Hades unleashed his kraken to destroy every sea creature along with every ship known. However, Freyja was not going to be a meal for the kraken, so instead she transformed herself into the ship so the ship could not be touched by any tentacle whatsoever. The power of Lucifer caused Freyja to become a piece of art within the ship for eternity.

Sergeant Waggit admired the woman as the art was so beautiful it reminded him of a woman that he was in love with a very long time ago. He knew the significance of this particular woman from readings of the past but had no idea that it was actually real. Not knowing the history behind Hades and his bride, Sergeant Waggit entered the ship that had a huge hole in the side and searched for things that he could find within this new land. There was a saying right next to the ship that said, "Who dares to lay hands on my bride shall perish forever into the depths of the darkness caverns for all eternity." Sergeant Waggit knew that the saying was referring to anybody that was to join forces with his bride that he had lost a very long time ago.

He also knew that by stepping inside the ship was significantly causing his body to instantly be perished forever, however, with holding the Rod of God, Hades cannot touch him as the power is too strong with lightness. Sergeant Waggit entered the ship and began searching everything for another stone, artifacts that he could use, or even weapons and ammunition. Along his journey inside the ship there were many chests that were locked that could be opened but with a special key. Sergeant Waggit must find this special key to unlock each chest in order to reveal what was inside them. He searched the entire ship for that special key but it was nowhere to be found in sight. Once the ship was cleared, Sergeant Waggit exited the ship on the other side and continued following the path to the next known location that would allow him to search for the key or other things that he needed. Sergeant Waggit stopped on the path as he saw a building that was in ruins, burned to the ground with fire all around it. He walked up to the door, opened it and entered the main lobby even though he knew that the building could crumble to pieces at any given moment. Sergeant Waggit searched the entire building floor by floor as it had over thirty floors. When he reached the twenty seventh floor, Sergeant Waggit noticed something that was in the middle of a room glowing brightly. He entered the room not knowing that it would be a trap. The door slammed shut behind him very quickly and a bunch of gargoyles came out of the vents from the air conditioning system. Using the double barrel shotgun, Sergeant Waggit began picking off each gargoyle one at a time until he had a huge pile of them stacked up all within the room. All of the gargoyles then disappeared leaving the artifact of something shiny in the middle room exposed for Sergeant Waggit to pick it up and examine it. He walked over to the artifact and picked it up. He noticed that it was a key of some sort with a skeleton for a head. To his understanding, Sergeant Waggit knew that a skeleton key most likely would open just about anything. Quickly, Sergeant Waggit stored the key away and began heading down all the stairs through this ruins building to the main entryway on the south side.

Once outside of the ruins building, Sergeant Waggit began heading back down the path to the damaged ship. Once arriving at the ship he re-entered through the back way and looked at the first chest. Sergeant Waggit took out the Skeleton key and put it into the lock of the chest. With a firm twist, the lock broke open. Sergeant Waggit removed the key from the lock and opened the chest. Inside the chest was a health pack and armor that could help him along his journey. Sergeant Waggit continued to search the rest of the ship and open every single chest exposing every little item that would help them along the way to include ammunition, food, and some other type of relics that he had no idea what they were for. Once all of the chests were open, Sergeant Waggit exited the ship and began to head back up the path to the building that he originally came from. he opened the door again to walk through the building but this time he just went to the back door and exited to get back on the path. Exploring the path a little further led Sergeant Waggit to another discovery of an interesting building. This next building was like a giant skyscraper with over one hundred floors. Sergeant Waggit stopped in front of the building and looked up at how tall it was. He wiped the sweat off his forehead and said out loud, "Fuck man. This is a tall building. It's going to take me forever to go through this son of a bitch. Oh well, I guess I got to start somewhere." Sergeant Waggit entered the main lobby of this new building and began claiming the stairs floor by floor searching for anything that he could use. Each floor that Sergeant Waggit explored had different types of little demons and gargoyles coming at him but nothing he could not handle. On the top floor of the building, Sergeant Waggit had to face a creature that was strange as he never saw this thing before. The creature was like a lizard and salamander combined with a demon head and it spit fire and acid all over the place. Sergeant Waggit fought this creature with all his might and every weapon that he could possibly use until it fell to its death in the middle of the room. The creature dropped a relic from its right hand onto the floor that was black in color. Sergeant Waggit walked over to the relic and picked it up.

He examined the relic and noticed that it looked like a crescent moon. The only thing that came to his mind at that moment was thinking of a witch or some form of being that served Hades but on a good point of view rather than a bad point of view. After securing the relic in his pouch, Sergeant Waggit headed down all the flight of stairs through every single level of the building and exited through the north side door to continue his journey along the narrow pathway.

Along his journey, Sergeant Waggit came across an old temple that was in ruins within the narrow path. He stopped to see what it looked like as it reminded him of a temple that he had visited when he was on a vacation when he served the United States Army. The temple was multiple buildings within a snowy mountain in the darkness of a realm being made out of stone. Candles lit the pathway to the main entryway along with red carpet laying on the path. Sergeant Waggit saw this amazing sight and said to himself, "I know I have seen this temple before and it looks the same with the exception that it has fire along the pathway as things were burning up and the temple looks to be in ruins. This was the place where mortal men and women would come to deal with their grievances and differences with fighting for their lives." Sergeant Waggit followed the pathway to the main door entryway. He stopped as there were two gargoyle stone statues outside on both the right and left side. As he stared into the eyes of the beasts, the gargoyles turned their heads towards Sergeant Waggit and made their eyes glow red as if they were possessed. Sergeant Waggit entered the main lobby area within the temple and began his search within the boundaries of the walls for anything that would help him on his way. While walking through the temple, Sergeant Waggit noticed that there were paintings on the glass that were stained similar to a church and artifacts of stone statues of people who were the temple's town spokesmen. Sergeant Waggit saw multiple little demon creatures that were floating nearby. As he approached the little demons, the little cute demon on his shoulder jumped off and turned into a large demon. With aiding Sergeant Waggit, the large demon attacked the little evil demons until they were all destroyed. Then the large demon turned back into the little cute demon and climbed back onto Sergeant Waggit's shoulder. Sergeant Waggit turned his head and looked at his cute little friend and said, "You are a good friend to have my little birdy... I mean demon." The little cute demon grunted in joy and smiled for Sergeant Waggit while staring into his eyes.

Sergeant Waggit continued searching the temple for items that would be useful during his journey. He stumbled across a statue that was completely made out of stone displaying a creature that was unheard of. The statue was a town spokesman with giant horns coming out of his head, had hooves for feet with the lower half of the legs bent backwards, and wore armor with a medallion that had a symbole on the face of the medallion that represented the light of the order within the temple. The statue was enormous in size and showed mussel outlines that made this creature look very strong. Sergeant Waggit kept an eye on the statue as he thought that it would come to life like the gargoyles outside did, but nothing happened. He continued to search the temple for items that he could use. Along the way, Sergeant Waggit noticed the same statue of the town spokesman within another room in the temple. He thought to himself, "Is it possible that this statue is following me?" Then he thought that the statue was just another spokesman within the temple's dwellings. As Sergeant Waggit searched more rooms within the temple he discovered even more of the statues. However, one of the rooms that he entered had twelve statues all lined up with six on one side and six on the other. All of the statues looked identical with the town's spokesman but each statue was different slightly within the armor or facial hair. At the end of the room after passing all twelve statues there was a seat that looked like something where an ambassador or king would sit within the temple. Near the seat was a rock-like structure sticking out of the ground that had divots or reversed buttons inside it. Sergeant Waggit placed his right hand onto the divots within the rock and noticed that they would make noise and line up a little indicating they were some form of activation key. He kept moving his hand around touching the buttons trying to make a unique key pattern with different noises. After multiple attempts, the key pattern noises stopped and all of a sudden a hologram appeared displaying what had happened long time ago within the temple. Sergeant Waggit watched the hologram and recorded it into his computer database. As he was watching the hologram, Sergeant Waggit noticed that all of the town's spokesmen we're running wild trying to hide from something but had no idea what it was. Then in the distance coming into the room was nothing more than a black figure like a cloud that was dark in the sky with electricity forming around it and spinning uncontrollably. This black figure must have been Hades himself in the form of a god displaying himself as the most evil presence within the temple. The black figure cast upon a spell within the towns spokesmen causing them to become nothing more than a stone figure. One of those town's spokesman sat down in the chair trying to gain immortal power to keep them from dying or turning into stone by this evil creature. However, the power that was within that chair was not strong enough to shield themselves from the evil presence within the dwellings of the temple. The black figure sent its body into the town's spokesman which then in turn made the being transformed into a very large beast and then in prisoned within a dungeon across the known universe. The very large beast was now considered the most evil dark guard of all.

Once the hologram stopped displaying, Sergeant Waggit believed that the dark black figure may still have its presence within the temple even though there was nothing there. Then all of a sudden, each of the town's spokesmen that was nothing more than stone statues, again to crumble the stone around the particular individuals making them display themselves as twelve guards within the temple. He took out the Rod of God and began to fight each of these guards one by one. The town's spokesmen guards were not very easy to fight as they wanted to do nothing but rip Sergeant Waggit to pieces. The town's spokesmen circled around Sergeant Waggit. Each of them lunged forward trying to catch Sergeant Waggit off guard in surprise attacks. After a long vigorous fight with all twelve towns spokesmen guards, Sergeant Waggit celebrated in defeat by collecting all of the dropped items that would help him in the next battle that he's about to encounter. He then saw that the room had destroyed a part of the wall just behind the seat causing a hole in the wall. Sergeant Waggit quickly collected all of the items and headed towards the wall and exited the temple's room to see where it would lead to. Just outside the hole in the wall, Sergeant Waggit noticed that he was back on the narrow path that would lead him to another location within the land that he is in. Sergeant Waggit continued to follow the pathway until he saw a strange structure that looked like an old mine shaft. With caution, Sergeant Waggit entered the old mine shaft in hopes that he would find something useful that would benefit his journey.

While inside the mine shaft, Sergeant Waggit noticed that the ground was full of cracks and had stones that were sharp on the ceiling that could come down at any given moments of notice. As Sergeant Waggit walked through the mine shaft, he took small steps around the cracks to keep from falling down into the mine. Along the pathway, there was a rock formation that Sergeant Waggit stumbled upon that began to crack. He said to himself, "Oh Shit. Wait, where do I remember this from?" Sergeant Waggit's weight was just enough to not allow the rock formation to crumble. He heard a loud crackle noise that came from the mine shaft that sounded like a dog bark. Then all of a sudden, one of the pointy rocks on the ceiling fell down crashing into the rock formation. Before Sergeant Waggit could get off the rock formation, the rock formation broke causing Sergeant Waggit to fall. He yelled out, "Ohhh... Fuuuuck!!!" Sergeant Waggit fell a long time through the hole that was broken up within the mine shaft. It seemed as if he fell for miles which could lead up to a dead stop in a pile of rubble or bounce off the floor. Near the end of the fall, Sergeant Waggit noticed that there was sand pouring out of the ground. He said to himself while staring at the sand, "Maybe the sand will make a slide for me and cushion my fall." At the end of the fall, Sergeant Waggit was brushed up against the sand and he then began to slide down the sand as if he was sliding down a sand dune.

After Sergeant Waggit had stopped moving within the sand, he got up out of the sand and stood up. He looked all around the area that he was at and saw a light coming from a rock in a wall. Sergeant Waggit picked up his belongings and headed over to the light coming from the rocks. He noticed that the light was coming from a small rock-like structure that he could crumble. Using the Rod of God, Sergeant Waggit was able to open up the wall enough so that he could fit through. Once the wall was open, Sergeant Waggit climbed through the wall to see nothing but a cool giant ball of fire in the unknown. Then all of a sudden, something shielded the light and made a noise. Sergeant Waggit took the Rod of God and used it to light up the area with a flame on the end similar to a torch. In front of his eyes, Sergeant Waggit noticed a creature of the deep that large in size and had three heads. He noticed that there were multiple torches along the walls of the area that he was standing in. With the cast of the Rod of God towards the torches, all of the torches lit up exposing light in all directions. Sergeant Waggit got a better glimpse of the creature that was standing in front of him. The creature was known as "Cerberus", a giant three headed vicious dog that stunk and had drool oozing out of its mouths like syrup coming out of a syrup dispenser. Sergeant Waggit knew that this creature could be beaten but he had no idea how to destroy it. On the creature's neck was a collar that had a chain applied to it. The creature ran up to Sergeant Waggit as fast as it could but before it could reach Sergeant Waggits location, the chain pulled tight causing the creature to stop in its tracks. Sergeant Waggit used all of his weapons to fight this creature until it was laying on the ground. As the creature was laying on the ground, Sergeant Waggit ran up to its belly and began to force the Rod of God upon it to stop the heart, however, the hyve was too thick and could not penetrate the rod through. The creature stood back up with Sergeant Waggit standing underneath its legs. The middle head looked down under its body to see Sergeant Waggit standing underneath. The creature then began to run around to expose Sergeant Waggit for a good meal. Sergeant Waggit continued to run with the creature to keep from being eaten. As he kept on running around, the chain that was attached to the creature's collar kept getting stuck on objects within the area. Sergeant Waggit noticed this and continued to make the creature run all around forcing the chain to become shorter and shorter as it kept on catching each object. Once the chain was snug tight and made the creature stand still as the chain had no more slack, Sergeant Waggit ran out in front of the creature. Cerberus, the three headed dog, began to bark horrendously towards Sergeant Waggit with spitting saliva at his feet. The rocks on the roof began to shake and then drop onto the creatures heads, causing the rock to penetrate through destroying each and every head.

After all of the heads to the creature were destroyed the creature fell to the ground. Sergeant Waggit noticed that there was a glowing object near one of the creature's necks. Sergeant Waggit ran up onto the creature to get a closer look. He saw the glowing object coming from the collar near one of the chain links. Sergeant Waggit went over to the collar and noticed that the glowing object was a stone. He took out his glove and retrieved the stone from the collar. Sergeant Waggit removed the Rod of God and placed the stone into the next slot that it would fit into. The rod once again changed colors to a bright orange with white spots. The new power that the rod was influenced with was the ability to stop any object in time from moving for a short period of time. Sergeant Waggit used his scanner to determine what stone he just collected. The computer system analyzed the findings and reported by saying, "The stone that was retrieved is known as the Crater Stone."

Sergeant Waggit felt good about finding this stone and he is now closer to finding the rest of the stones within his journey. He climbed down the creature known as Cerberus and began searching for a portal of a way out. There was nothing in sight to escape within except for volcano chambers.

Sergeant Waggit headed over to one of the volcano chambers that was empty and began following it to find a way out. He ran into a tube that looked like it led to a surface as there was a little light at the top. Sergeant Waggit began climbing the walls of the volcano tube to reach the top, even though it is miles away. All of a sudden, lava started to form underneath the volcano tube and slowly reached Sergeant Waggit's location. Sergeant Waggit cast a power from the Rod of God to create ice onto the lava. In return, the ice turned into steam and rushed past Sergeant Waggit as if a huge ventilation system was turned on. Sergeant Waggit lost his grip and began floating through the volcano tube all the way to the top. Once outside the volcano tube, Sergeant Waggit fell down the side of the mountain top and landed into a hay pit. He said to himself, "Wow, that was fuck'n crazy." Sergeant Waggit got up and began heading away from the mountain top in search for any other stones or useful items that he could use.

CHAPTER NINE

The Pyroclastic Cloud Disaster

During the descent down a hill past the mountain range area, Sergeant Waggit thought that he was clear from the volcano blast area but had no idea of the exact location that he was within. As he was continuing his search for other items Sergeant Waggit heard a loud rumbling sound and then all of a sudden the ground began to shake horrendously. The top of the mountain blew its top exposing the largest volcano in the world of the underground to cause a giant pyroclastic cloud. Sergeant Waggit stomped in his tracks and turned around quickly to see what happened. To his eyes, Sergeant Waggit saw a giant cloud of smoking debris with lots of dust and Ash coming down right off the mountain flowing towards his direction. Without mercy, Sergeant Waggit turned back around and began to run as fast as he could to get away from this giant cloud of dust and ash. The cloud of dust and ash with all the debris coming down the mountain became more eruptive as the volcano continued to pump out more smoke every second. Within a few minutes after running from the pyroclastic cloud, Sergeant Waggit ended up engulfed with the cloud around his entire existing area.

Running as fast as he could so the ash and debris does not get into the computer systems within his suit, Sergeant Waggit noticed an abandoned structure nearby. He ran over to the structure to shield his suit and computer system from the ash that can harmfully destroy it within a matter of seconds. Once entering the abandoned structure, Sergeant Waggit noticed that there were markings within the walls. He used his computer system to analyze the markings to determine exactly what they were. the markings on the wall were nothing more than constellations within space given an existent location of something most evil of a presence that exists within that point. Sergeant Waggit said to himself, "Could it be the location where Hades is actually hiding?" After getting a full skin of all of the constellational drawings and waiting for the pyroclastic cloud to kind of calm down a little, Sergeant Waggit left the abandoned structure and began to head out looking for things that he can use along his journey.

Along his way around the grounds surrounded by the ash and dark thick clouds of mush coming from the mountain, Sergeant Waggit noticed some things that were on the ground that allowed him to shield himself from the ash that could damage his computer system. However, it was too late for the weapon systems that he had other than the Rod of God as the muzzles of each weapon was full of Ash and debris preventing them from functioning properly. Demons alert on the grounds in front of Sergeant Waggit's path waiting for him to cross their lines. Not knowing that the weapons could be damaged due to the dust and debris within the cloud, Sergeant Waggit took out his heavy cannon rifle and squeezed the trigger. With hoping that the rifle would actually fire around, Sergeant Waggit was surprised when all he heard was a click as the weapon jammed up due to the dust and debris within the cloud. Of course Sergeant Waggit was not going to give up and began to take the weapon and slam it onto the ground hard to try to shake out such a mess that caused it to jam up. Within moments the demons in front of Sergeant Waggit were within arm's reach and ready to pounce at any moments of notice. As there was no time to take out another weapon for any kind of attack, Sergeant Waggit grabbed seismic charges and threw them towards the demons. One by one each demon stepped onto a charge allowing it to explode similar to a mine detonating within the grounds. All the demons perished within the area allowing the pathway to be cleared for Sergeant Waggit to continue his search in the need of objects that helps his journey experience.

After traveling through the pyroclastic

cloud for a few miles now, Sergeant Waggit was wondering if he was ever going to find anything as the cloud was so thick that merely anything around it was difficult to see. Then as there was no luck for miles all of a sudden there was a bright shiny object lying on the ground. Sergeant Waggit ran over to the object as quick as he could to see what it was just to find out it was nothing but a mirage. Sergeant Waggit stomped in his tracks and yelled out, "Son of a Bitch!!" He continued to run as quickly as he could through the thick cloud of dust and debris trying to locate objects that could help him along his way. Once again there was not anything found within the reach of his grasp as it was so dark and so difficult to see the ground but then all of a sudden Sergeant Waggit got a wonderful idea. He reached back and got the Rod of God out and decided to use it as a torch but with a spell cast upon it that would cause a shield. Sergeant Waggit didn't know whether it was going to work or not but after casting the spell and lighting the torch on the end of the Rod of God it indeed helped his path. Holding the Rod of God high above his head, Sergeant Waggit was able to see lots of area around him and acknowledge whether there was something there or not. The rod cast a spell strong enough to shield the cloud around him and not allow it to touch his weapons, his suit, nor either have him breathe it.

Once a couple more hours had passed and

more demons were fought off that lurked within the pathway that Sergeant Waggit was walking through, Sergeant Waggit noticed that there was a mine that was nearby. He began to head in the direction where the mine was trying to get out of the cloud even though he can see in some form of a distance in front of him due to the rod that he's holding. Once out of the pyroclastic cloud and clear within the mine, Sergeant Waggit saw something that was black even though the light was on it. He ran over to see what it was and discovered that it was merely nothing but a dark, black chest. Sergeant Waggit used the Rod of God to pry open the black chest. To his surprise, inside the chest was a new weapon and Sergeant Waggit's eyes began to grow in size as he was so surprised and happy. He reached into this black chest and took out the weapon with a firm grip. While holding an enormous sized weapon in front of him, Sergeant Waggit was glad that he had found a large flamethrower. This new weapon not only would be good to light a path up but it would also be good to burn anything to a stake within a fifty foot radius around his direction of where he would stand. As Sergeant Waggit began his search within this mine, he noticed that there were some creatures that were hanging on the ceiling. Sergeant Waggit reached down and picked up a rock and chucked it and one of the creatures that was hanging from the ceiling. The creature flew down and Sergeant Waggit was able to get a closer look. He noticed that they were vampire bats that look like they were on steroids. These beds were totally insane as they were black and very large in size. One bat was big enough to carry off a human being to any known location anywhere. Along with that he also noticed that the fangs that these things had were totally huge. Each fang was long enough to be the length of a number two pencil. The only thing that these vampire bats were afraid of was fire. Sergeant Waggit lit up the flamethrower and began to torch those bastards from head to toe. some of the vampire bats fell from the ceiling onto the ground to their death while other vampire bats saw that he had nothing but fear coming towards them and they fled from the heat and fire coming out of the barrel of the flamethrower.

The tunnel within the mine was now clear from any creature that lured within the ceiling or walls. Sergeant Waggit continued his search to see if he could find any stones but couldn't find any and he was getting so upset. Then a wall crashed down next to him exposing something that was very peculiar. Sergeant Waggit noticed an old abandoned mine track that would lead him to somewhere within the mine that could give him what he needed, the rest of the stones.

CHAPTER TEN

Track Ahead Looks Good

Climbing through the newly opened hole was not exactly easy as it looked. Sergeant Waggit struggled to climb through the hole trying not to collapse it on top of him or damage any part of his suit. As he climbed through the hole in the wall, Sergeant Waggit looked down the old abandoned track and saw that there was a minecart sitting on it. He put his right hand onto his chin and said to himself, "I wonder where this track leads and if they can lead me out of this forbidden place and also along the way possibly find what I'm looking for." Sergeant Waggit climbed into the minecart and released the break. The minecart began to slowly move forward along the tracks bumping side to side as the track was slightly uneven. The minecart began to speed up uncontrollably. Sergeant Waggit pulled the lover to apply the brakes to the wheels so that the minecart could slow down. Sparks flew all over the place as the brakes were being applied to the wheels then all of a sudden the handle snapped off causing the brakes to fail. Sergeant Waggit lift the broken handle to his face and said to himself out loud, "Fuck!!" While holding on with both his hands on each side of the minecart, Sergeant Waggit kept a firm grip to keep himself from falling out as the minecart was speeding up to a speed of around sixty mile per hour. The track was beginning to turn to the left slightly and still heading downward causing the mine cart to speed up even faster. Then after a moment or so, the track decided to go upward motion causing the minecart to slow down but not stop as it was still moving in a quick motion. Up over the horizon of the track looked as if it was going to go back down. Sergeant Waggit noticed that there was a valley out there which was an open area that had a red glow tint to it. The minecart reached the top of the tracks and then began a descent into a really steep cliff. Sergeant Waggit held on with all his might and yelled out, "Ohhhh Fuuuck!!!" The minecart headed down the tracks with an extreme quick motion bumping side to side extremely fast causing it to shutter and vibrate to the most extreme feeling of all.

The minecart sped up to an astonishing speed of a round one-hundred miles per hour. As the track bowed down near the glow that was below in a valley, Sergeant Waggit got a glimpse of what was underneath him. He gripped the society even harder as he did not want to fall off since there was nothing but boiling magma below the tracks. The cart then came up to a high motion as it was speeding extremely fast but now in an upper direction. Sergeant Waggit noticed that the track ahead was broken and part of it was just sunk underneath the other part. With blind luck, the minecart flew off the top of the track and landed on the other track just on the other side which was only about a two-foot difference and caused it to bounce around but not fall off the tracks. As the minecart was squealing with noise as the wheels were heating up and causing the bearings to squeal loudly with a screeching type bird noise, the noise began to echo within the walls of the canyon inside the mine. As the minecart kept on moving with an extreme speed and going up and down on the tracks speeding up and slowing down but continuing on its path, the sound from the screeching bearing noise began to shake ceiling structures making them collapse and fall into the magma below. a very large structure that was above the tracks fell down and broke through the track exposing a huge gap in between the tracks. Sergeant Waggit became extremely feared as he might think the minecart may plunged directly into the magma below. However, the tracks began to head up in an upward direction towards where Sergeant Waggit needed to be, where the track was broken and speeding around seventy miles per hour. Right at the moment that the minecart left the track, it sailed through the air just flying as if it had wings applied to it. Then right at the very end the front wheels slammed down onto the other side of the track that was still together and the back wheels bounced really hard as they went underneath the track and then popped onto the track. The minecart shuttered and slid around as if it was trying to bounce off of the track up onto two wheels on the right hand side. Sergeant Waggit leaned his entire body and his gear all the way to the left hoping that the minecart would fall back down onto the tracks. Within moments the minecart fell back on the tracks slamming back and forth causing it to shake the entire track.

As the minecart continued on its path along the tracks heading to somewhere within the mine and making the most screeching sound possible with struggling to stay on the track by bouncing left and right, Sergeant Waggit noticed that the track behind him began to crumble and fall into the magma below. He kept an eye on the track as it kept falling in crumbling and getting closer to the minecart. The minecart was still speeding at a very high rate heading any downward motion causing it to speed up faster and faster. Even though the minecart continued to speed up, the track behind the cart continued to crumble and fall to the depths below where the magma was boiling, burning up everything that could just fall into it. And now got to the point where the track right behind the minecart was collapsing at the back wheels causing the minecart to really shake and bounce all over the place. Sergeant Waggit now feared that the track would collapse underneath him and he would have to bail off and run down the tracks as fast as he could so he would not fall into the magma below. Right at the last moment right before the minecart would collapse off the tracks and fall into the magma below, the minecart reached a strong piece of land where the tracks would not fall and within seconds of the minecart tipping backwards almost ready to fall it bounced harshly forward tipping on the front two wheels holding a nosedive for a very long distance. Sergeant Waggit was happy the fact that he did not fall to his death into the boiling magma below, however, he was now extremely feared for the fact that he might fall out of the minecart and get run over by the minecart at extreme speeds. Sergeant Waggit ran to the back of the minecart and jumped up and down as hard as he could causing the rear of it to fall down. Once the minecart was back on all four wheels and screeching down the tracks as fast as it could, the tracks then dipped back down and extreme steep Canyon causing the minecart to speed up with immense speed of over one-hundred fifty miles per hour. Sergeant Waggit looked ahead where the track was leading him and noticed that part of the track was submerged in the magma that was below. The tracks however were not melted but were glowing very red as if it was getting ready to melt. Sergeant Waggit ducked down into the minecart and covered his whole body to prevent any of the magma from coming in contact with him as the cart was getting ready to speed right through it. After a few seconds the minecart slammed right into the magma that was covering over the rail wheels and began to spray in an outward direction like if they were waves spraying an hour direction on a boat in a lake.

Once the minecart was out of the location of where the tracks were dipped down and heading around the corner, Sergeant Waggit stood up in the cart and looked over the side to see if the wheels were still intact as there was a very loud noise coming from that area. The wheels were definitely intact however they were glowing so red and the bearings were completely seized up but causing the wheels to just slide along the tracks as they were still spinning because of the steel being melted. Then near the end of the track there was a warning sign that had stated that the track ended there. Sergeant Waggit had to think of something very quickly to make him be able to get off this minecart as quickly as he could and safely without destroying anything or damaging any part of his suit or weapons that he had. Then with a blink of an eye, Sergeant Waggit reached into his utility pouch and removed some rope that he had. He took the broken handle that was for the brakes of the minecart and tied it to the end of the rope. Then, Sergeant Waggit tied the other end of the rope around his waist. With a quick throw of the handle, the handle and rope flew into a wide open area. Sergeant Waggit hoped that the handle would grab something that could hold in place so he could escape the uncontrolled minecart. As the minecart was nearing its last descent to its destruction at the end of the track, the handle bounced on the wooden ties and then lodged itself underneath one of the wooden ties. Sergeant Waggitflew up in the air as the rope became extremely tight and pulled him right out of the minecart. Within seconds after floating through the air, gravity pulled Sergeant Waggit back down and slammed him into the track. The minecart then smashed into the end sign and crashed into a wall exposing another area within the mine that could be beneficial but also dangerous the same time.

Sergeant Waggit stood up and shook off all the dust that was on him from falling onto the tracks. He secured all of his weapons and gear and headed over to where the minecart had crashed into the nearby wall. With a quick glimpse of what was on the other side of the wall, Sergeant Waggit noticed something that was glowing bright and had a good feeling that it could be something he was looking for. He climbed through the wall and into the structure that was just on the other side of the wall and tried to look to see where the glow was coming from. It was extremely bright but not near his grasp but rather a high up distance inside of a round tube. Sergeant Waggit noticed that once again he was standing inside a volcano tube but this time it was a little different. There were no stones or anything among the walls and the floor was extremely thick that he could stand on it without falling through. Using his rope and some other tools that could help him climb, Sergeant Waggit began to ascend to the location where the bright gym lurked. While Sergeant Waggit was climbing up a volcano tube, he stopped for a moment and noticed that there was a hole in the wall that was big enough to fit something small. With seeing a pair of eyes within the hole, Sergeant Waggit got curious and wanted to look at it a little bit closer. All of a sudden, a goblin climbed out of the wall jumping at Sergeant Waggit trying to claw him. Sergeant Waggit swung out of the way enough to where the goblin would fall to its death falling all the way down the tube. He then continued to go up the volcano tube as quickly as he could to reach what he saw that was nearing his location. More goblins began to climb out of other holes that were within the tube and began to attack Sergeant Waggit. Most of the goblins fell to their death as Sergeant Waggit knocked them all around but other ones began to claw at the suit that he was wearing. With a quick motion of grabbing the Rod of God, Sergeant Waggit quickly used it to light up a fire which caused all the goblins to be scared and flee to their own death as they pushed away from the ball of flame at the end of the Rod of God.

Once all of the goblins had failed to their

death and climbed just a little bit farther up, Sergeant Waggitreached the glowing gem which he had noticed was stuck in the side of the volcano tube. With a quick motion using a pick, Sergeant Waggit freed the stone that was stuck in the tube. Using his glove he picked up the stone and put it onto the Rod of God. The stone adapted to the rod and once again, changing the color and structure of what it looked like giving it even more power than it originally had. Sergeant Waggit's computer system within his helmet acknowledged that the stone that was picked up was known as the ice stone. The new stone attached to the Rod of God gave Sergeant Waggit the ability to apply ice to anything including lava. After just a few moments from retrieving the new stone lava began to swarm at the bottom of the volcano tube. Within seconds the lava rose to a depth that would be right just underneath Sergeant Waggit's feet. Sergeant Waggit pointed the Rod of God towards the magma just below his feet and said out loud with a loud voice, "Let's see if this fuck'n works!" Then he activated the rod and allowed it to dump ice all over the magma. By doing this the ice melted very quickly and turned into a big bowl of steam which then started blowing past Sergeant Waggit with a very strong current. As the steam was passing past Sergeant Waggit, he could no longer hold his grip on the side of the volcano tube and let go. The steam allowed him to flow through the tube that extreme speeds all the way up until he popped out of the volcano. Just below his location in mid-air, Sergeant Waggit noticed the minecart that he rode in. He made himself fall down as fast as he could so he can fall into the minecart. Then with a quick motion of falling to the ground, the minecart slammed onto the outside of the volcano mountain and began to descend the mountain side until he reached a tunnel. The tunnel was extremely long and dark but light at the other end. The minecart rolled all the way through the tunnel and stopped within a few feet from the other end exposing a unique surrounding area. Sergeant Waggit looked around and noticed that the area he was in looked similar to a courtroom where there were chairs outside within a pillar and a gavel was left on a table nearby one of the chairs in the middle.

CHAPTER ELEVEN

Court of the Dead

The outside courtroom known as the Court of the Dead was ruled by nine individuals that were under the supervision of Hades. Sergeant Waggit looked around the courtroom that was outdoor and saw that the room had nine chairs. There were four chairs on each side of the room in a u-shape formation along with a ninth chair right in the middle at the back of the room. A glowing light was shining within the middle of the four chairs which was also the middle of the courtroom platform. With curiosity, Sergeant Waggit walked over to the glowing light to see what it was. After stepping on top of where the glowing light was, a force field wrapped around Sergeant Waggit preventing him from moving in any direction. He got very disturbed for the fact that he could not move and was trying to figure out any possible way to get out of this force field. While Sergeant Waggit was trying to escape the force field, he began to notice that there were skeleton-like figures wearing cloaks appeared on each of the chairs with the exception of the middle chair still being dormant and silent. Eight skeleton-like figures were all standing in front of their chairs and then took a seat into each one. Sergeant Waggit looked over at one of the skeleton-like figures and asked, "Who or what are you?" The skeleton-like figure to the right in the second chair responded by saying, "We are the judges of Hades to rule the lands and give justice to all that stands within." Sergeant Waggit then asked another question by saying, "If you all are judges and there seems to only be eight of them then who sits in the throne or that chair right in the middle?" The skeleton-like figure pointed towards the middle chair and looked directly at Sergeant Waggit and began to say, "That chair belongs to the head judge which has the final say and final rule over the land by the hand of Hades."

As Sergeant Waggit was still trapped within the force field he began to become nervous, noticing that eight skeleton-like figures known as judges within the kingdom of Hades were staring at him. Sergeant Waggit then set out loud to all the judges to hear his voice, "Set me free from this so-called force field and I'll do anything that you asked me to do!" One of the skeleton-like figure judges was about to say something but then there was a voice that appeared behind Sergeant Waggit that said loudly, "SILENCE!!" The ninth skeleton-like judge walked from behind to in front of Sergeant Waggit to show who he really was. The ninth judge was not just black and color and skeleton-like figure, but also had a unique armor set that it was wearing to make it more distinctive than the other judges. The armor of the judge was black in color with a shiny metal tint to it signifying that the metal was made of a valuable substance. The judge had a black cape applied to his back that had gold pinstriping all the way around it signifying that he was an important figure within the ruling of the land of Hades. The judge had red eyes that glowed as if they had fire within them and his helmet was uniquely shaped like a wedge and had sharp pointy ears that stuck straight up along with horns that came out the side signifying these strength levels of him being with the dead. Staring into Sergeant Waggit's soul, the judge said with a strong crisp voice, "You are Sergeant Waggit, a defied soldier and strong being that has lost his will to survive within the land of Hades and is hereby to be challenged within the justice system of Hades." Sergeant Waggit looked at the judge and said with a calm voice, "Who... Who are you?" The judge nodded and then said, "I am Sadon, the great and noble black knight of the court of the dead."

Sadon turned around away from Sergeant Waggit and waddled himself over to his noble chair and sat down gracefully. He looked directly at Sergeant Waggit and said, "You are here to face your good and evil side. All of us can look into your soul and see exactly who you are and what your purpose is here. In order to continue past our courtroom, you will have to pass several tests. Each test will challenge your mind and strength which in turn can either strengthen your mind or strengthen our minds. The choices are all up to you to decide as we dig deep into your soul." Sergeant Waggit tried the best that he could to keep these judges from banishing him to the deaths of the Hades lairs into the death of all doom. The challenge began with each and every judge staring into Sergeant Waggit's soul. In front of his eyes, Sergeant Waggit noticed a large display similar to a hologram that displayed whatever the judges were seeing within his soul. One by one each judge pierced deep into Sergeant Waggit's soul in the search for good and bad trying to pinpoint only evil resemblance of himself. The display showed memories of Sergeant Waggit when he was being evil and destructive to everything. Of course Sergeant Waggit was going to resist the temptation of the evil side of him by trying to add in the good side of him. The judges dug deeper and harder to keep Sergeant Waggit from displaying anything that was good and his heart. Sergeant Waggit gripped his hands until they were a strong fists to resist the temptation of displaying nothing but evil. The more he resisted and the more temptation occurred within his mind the more evil was displayed upon the hologram like vision set.

After multiple attempts to pull out all the

evil within his soul, the judges were getting stronger by the minute and becoming more than a judge and more of a immortal being. In order for Sergeant Waggit to defeat and win victory against this court of the dead, he needed to display a good side and keep it good for all time and eliminate the evil within. Sergeant Waggit began to think extremely hard thoughts about everything he did that was nothing but good. He thought about when he was in the service and serving his country with pride and the understanding of the good presence that he did to help all citizens that deserved freedom. Sergeant Waggit then began to think about all the good stuff he did with his family and understanding the wellness and kindness that he provided for his children. Along with all of the goodness that he was trying to share, Sergeant Waggit also thought about the ten years that he had spent living with the few people that survived Earth before it was destroyed within the walls of a secured building upon a moon in the Andromeda Galaxy. Emotionally, Sergeant Waggit became angry with his thoughts towards these judges and knew that they were becoming stronger because of his evil side to him which he had doubts about knowing whether that was the only thing that was going to be shed out. Instead Sergeant Waggit pursued his thoughts to be as good as possible but with anger and remorse towards these judges that wanted nothing more than to grow on his fears and strengthen themselves from his evil. Sergeant

Waggit reached his arms behind him, his shoulders as strong as he could as the force field was preventing him from doing so and took out the Rod of God. Sergeant Waggit placed it into his hands where he could hold it steady with a firm grip. While holding onto the Rod of God with all his might, Sergeant Waggit began to yell out, "You can see into my soul but you don't own it!! You shall die now!!" Sergeant Waggit got enough strength within his body from fighting against the judges power and regained his power to overcome the force field and caused it to collapse. He then took the rod and activated it with the power to disintegrate anything. As the rod was being pointed towards each of the judges that were sitting on the sides, Sergeant Waggit began to use the weapon against them, vanishing them into dust. After destroying all eight of the judges on the sides, the only judge that Sergeant Waggit had to deal with now was the Black Knight judge. He knew it was not going to be easy and knew that it was going to be a big fight until the end.

Sergeant Waggit approached the last judge that was sitting in the main chair. The judge applied a force field around him and stood up to fight him for his soul. Sergeant Waggit refused the judge from taking his soul and pushed him to the limits. While Sergeant Waggit was screaming in terror bent over backwards with the power being drained out of his body from the last judge trying to suck every piece of his soul away, he managed to pretend that he was going to be at his side and allow the judge to stop what he's doing. For a second there Sergeant Waggit thought that everything was all over and that he could destroy this judge at once but to his knowledge that was not what was going to happen. The judge turned to his side and then turned back with his hands forcing towards Sergeant Waggit causing a huge wind to overcome the area. Sergeant Waggit flew backwards and landed on the ground banging his head up against a huge rock. The Black Knight judge approached Sergeant Waggit and looked down at him. He said with gazing upon his body, "Wait, I've seen this before in a vision that you had that I was seeking through your soul. I do know that this is the end of you now. Yes, you were lying exactly where you are and for me I stand right here in front of you next to your feet and I'm supposed to say something. I say, even though you shed good but your evil outweighs everything and you will be one of us. You will bow to Hades' feet." Sergeant Waggit then turned his head and looked at the Black Knight judge. The judge then began to look in sorrow and said, "No, no this isn't right. This can't be right. You were dead." Sergeant Waggit stood up and faced the Black Knight judge. The judge stood back from him and said out loud, "Get away from me at once!" Sergeant Waggit then said to the knight, "Why are you scared? You afraid of something?" The judge then said with a feared look, "It's a trick isn't it!" Sergeant Waggit then said, "You think that you can have anything that you want including myself but today that is not going to happen." The Black Knight judge looked Sergeant Waggit up and down and then said with an angry tone, "You well give me your soul now!!" Sergeant Waggit yelled back to the judge, "You cannot have my fuck'n soul!!!" The Black Knight judge then reached out and forced his hand onto Sergeant Waggit's chest trying to force his soul from his body. Having all the power within his might the rod began to light up every single stone one by one until all of the stones were lit up. Sergeant Waggit then felt a power within him channel through his arms into the Rod of God forcing it to glow a bright spectrum color. The energy applied to the rod burst out onto the judge causing him to shed light from within his own helmet. Then after a little bit of time of the light piercing through the judge and Sergeant Waggit shedding out as much anger as he possibly could that he had within his soul, the Black Knight judge exploded throwing Sergeant Waggit backwards across the courtyard.

Sergeant Waggit stood up and looked around to see what just happened. He noticed that the judge was no longer there and everything was destroyed including all the chairs. Sergeant Waggit picked up the Rod of God that had fallen onto the ground after he flew backwards. He was about to put it away but then he stopped to look at it. Sergeant Waggit said to himself while staring at the Rod of God, "What was that? I didn't think I had that kind of power within me. Fuck, I wish I had that kind of power all the time." Sergeant Waggit then stored away the Rod of God and picked up some things out of his way that were preventing him from walking forward and got a glimpse of where the chairs were. He noticed that there was something glowing where the Black Knight judge sat before. Sergeant Waggit walked over to where the chair was and noticed that the glowing object was a stone. He took out his glove and put it on to ensure that his hands would not be destroyed from some stone. Reaching down through the rebel, Sergeant Waggit recovered the lost stone. While holding the stone in one hand, Sergeant Waggit removed the Rod of God from his back with the other hand. Very carefully, he applied the stone to the rod and the rod accepted it. A new power was applied to the rod causing it to change structure and color once again. His computer system analyzed the stone and mentioned that it was known as the Dark Matter Stone. The computer system said, "The stone that you had found is known as the Dark Matter Stone. This Stone will give you the ability to walk through walls and also make yourself cloaked invisibility temporarily from any enemy." Sergeant Waggit said to himself, "Now, that is some cool shit... walk through walls... and be invisible. Hell yeah!" Sergeant Waggit then put away the Rod of God and left the courtyard to find something else and hope to look for more stones along his way.

CHAPTER TWELVE

Escape the Sandworm

Along his journey through a deep thick woods full of multiple different types of trees and rubbish, Sergeant Waggit finally was away far enough from the courtyard. He noticed that there was a hill that was a ways away and decided to head that direction. Climbing the hill was not very easy as it was really steep like a mountain grade type. Sergeant Waggit climbed all the way up the hill to the very top and then walked across the plateau at the top of the hill. He was not paying attention very well to his footing and slipped down a tunnel that let him into the hillside. With dirt and debris falling with him as he was sliding down a tunnel, Sergeant Waggit was feared to know where this tunnel would lead him to. After a long slide, Sergeant Waggit fell out of the tunnel onto the ground which had a strange texture to it. Sergeant Waggit stood up onto this ground within the hill and said to himself, "Well, that was a long fall all the way down from the top of the hill now down to inside it where it's dark and seems to be wet. Also, what the fuck is on the ground to make it have a strange texture?" Sergeant Waggit removed the Rod of God from his back and stabbed it onto the ground. The ground began to move as if there was an earthquake or something. After a few minutes of moving the ground stopped moving. Sergeant Waggit took the Rod of God and stabbed the ground again. The ground moved again as if there was another earthquake. Sergeant Waggit said to himself, "What the fuck!... Wait, it can't be." Sergeant Waggit looked ahead and saw light at the end of where he was standing. The light looked like it was becoming thinner and thinner by the minutes. Using his computer system, Sergeant Waggit zoomed in to see what was at the end of whatever he was in and discovered there were teeth. He then said to himself out loud, "Oh Shit! I'm in the belly of a sandworm!... I think!"

Sergeant Waggit began to run towards the light so he could get out of the belly of this monster. Along his way while he was running, bats came swarming down in front of him trying to claw at his body suit and bite at his face. Sergeant Waggit took out his flamethrower and began to burn old bats that were coming in his area. The bats saw the flame and diverted around it so they would not get burned up. Then dead soldiers began to climb out of the ground and follow him around. The soldiers picked up stones and sticks and chucked it at Sergeant Waggit trying to hit him and knock him down. Sergeant Waggit turned around and used the flamethrower to burn everything that was coming at him. Then he took out the Rod of God and used it to cloak himself. The dead soldiers stopped and looked all around to find Sergeant Waggit but had no luck in finding him. The dead soldiers then stopped their pursuit for Sergeant Waggit and went back into the ground. The cloaking ability from the Rod of God stopped and allowed Sergeant Waggit to be exposed as himself again. Sergeant Waggit then said to himself, "That was… Awesome!" He turned around and continued to run towards the light that was emitting from the other end.

As Sergeant Waggit continued to run through a sandworm monster, he stopped in his tracks as he saw a box on the side that had a chain wrapped around it with a lock. Sergeant Waggit took out every key that he had that he kept from the mushroom kingdom a while back and used them on the lock attached to the chains. The last key turned all the gears within the lock and allowed the locking mechanism to release popping the base of the lock down unlocking the lock from the chains. Sergeant Waggit removed the lock from the chains and took the chains off the box. He grabbed the top of the box, lifted it above his head, and placed it on the ground next to him. Sergeant Waggit looked into the box and saw that there was something in there but covered with some kind of mist. He moved his hands across the mist and saw something that could aid him. Sergeant Waggit reached into the box and removed a very unique tube with a belt of grenades. He got to looking at the tube and noticed that it was a grenade launcher attachment for his flamethrower. With a quick motion as he was short on time, Sergeant Waggit attached the grenade launcher to the flamethrower that he had and strapped the belt of grenades to his chest.

Sergeant Waggit continued to run as quickly as he could through the sandworm monster's belly hoping that the opening was not going to shut anytime soon. more bats came flying down towards him along with small demons and spiders climbing out of the walls. For mass destruction, Sergeant Waggit decided to try out the new granite launcher and pumped a few rounds off destroying the little demons and spiders. The explosions caused the warm to shake even more as if it was a massive earthquake. The opening began to close even faster than was expected. Sergeant Waggit ran as fast as he could as he was getting extremely close to the opening. He noticed that the opening was not just the end of a tunnel but the actual head and mouth of the sandworm monster. With seconds to spare, Sergeant Waggit lunged his body through the opening leading him to just outside of the sandworm monster's mouth. Right at the moment that his foot was just clearing the sandworm monster's mouth, within a couple inches of clearance the mouth shut leaving Sergeant Waggit free from injury.

Sergeant Waggit turned around to look at the monster and shot some flame out from the flamethrower to shed some light in the tunnel. The sandworm monster had a disturbing face with multiple different spikes upon it and red tentacles coming out where normally there would be eyes. Along with the disturbing look, the mouth had drool around it and lots of blood as it had devoured multiple victims along its path digging through the hillside. The sandborn monster began to go through the tunnels under the ground towards Sergeant Waggit. Sergeant Waggit saw that this sandworm monster began to come his direction and he put away his flamethrower. Sergeant Waggit began to run as fast as he could through the tunnels inside the hill. The sandworm monster chased Sergeant Waggit through the tunnels opening and closing its mouth trying to eat him. As Sergeant Waggit was running through the tunnels, he started to see that it was more like a maze. He kept running all around trying to find some form of shelter but had no idea of where one would be. After running for almost thirty minutes trying to get away from this sandworm monster, Sergeant Waggit noticed a small hole in the wall that he could possibly fit in. He stomped at the hole and began to climb into it trying to pull his feet into the hole the best that he could. Right at the very last second of pulling his feet in, just as Sergeant Waggit was able to clear his feet from the tunnel into the hole, the sandworm monster blue past him raging through the tunnels with a tremendous speed. Sergeant Waggit then claimed out of the hole that was in the wall and began to run after the sandworm monster in the search for some type of exit. After running for a very long time, the sandworm monster banging its tail against the walls caused a small opening that led to another tunnel. Sergeant Waggit ran through the opening into the next tunnel nearby and began to run as fast as he could to get away from the sandworm monster. The sandworm monster noticed that Sergeant Waggit had entered another tunnel by seeking out his scent. As the sandworm monster came up to the opening it turned and broke through it until the sandworm monster was in the other tunnel. Sergeant Waggit continued running and then all of a sudden the tunnel came to an end where it was open to a huge valley that had a long far drop all the way down into a lava pit. Sergeant Waggit didn't know where to go and thought maybe he can just run back down the tunnel to find another way out.

As Sergeant Waggit began running down the tunnel, he heard the noise of dirt crumbling and stones falling. Then all of a sudden, Sergeant Waggit saw the sandworm monster heading down the tunnel directly at him. Sergeant Waggit yelled out, "Fuck, this fucker will not leave me alone!!" Sergeant Waggit turned around and ran to the opening once again where the lava pit was below. As the sandworm monster continued on its approach, Sergeant Waggit got a brilliant idea and decided to wait for the monster to arrive on scene. Right when the sandworm monster was about to come in contact with Sergeant Waggit at the opening of the tunnel with its mouth wide open as it is ready to eat, Sergeant Waggit took out his rope and saw a tree branch sticking out of the wall next to the tunnel. He tied one end of the rope to the tree branch and wrapped the other part around his waist. Sergeant Waggit then swung his body across hoping that the tree branch would hold him so that he would not be in the tunnel anymore. The sandworm monster then blew out of the tunnel as fast as it could trying to bite Sergeant Waggit and then fell into the lava below. Sergeant Waggit watched the sandworm monster splash into the lava killing it at once. He then swung himself back around to try to get back into the tunnel. Right when Sergeant Waggit was able to get back into the tunnel, the tree branch broke off and fell into the lava below. Sergeant Waggit was so thankful that the tree branch did not break while he was on it.

Sergeant Waggit then ran down the tunnel looking for an exit. On the right side of the tunnel before it ended, Sergeant Waggit noticed a ladder that was attached to the side. He began to climb the ladder and reached the top where there was some form of hatch. With a couple turns of a knob within the hatch, Sergeant Waggit was able to pop it open. Light appeared as the hatch opened to the exterior of the hillside. Sergeant Waggit climbed out of the hatch and began to head down the hill. When he reached the bottom of the hill Sergeant Waggit stopped in his tracks. He said to himself, "That was one crazy maze." Sergeant Waggit then continued on foot past the hill looking for more stones and anything else that can help him along the way.

CHAPTER THIRTEEN

The Ferryman

The day was bright as the light from the sun or a terrarium within the underground that was shining upon the lands within the area that Sergeant Waggit was wandering through. Sergeant Waggit could see for up to a mile ahead of him as it was all clear with a nice blue sky. Within seconds, dark thick black clouds began to rush around the area in front of Sergeant Waggit. As he stopped really fast to see what was happening, Sergeant Waggit watched the clouds form over something he had no idea what was. Taking many precautions, Sergeant Waggit continued to walk down the lands and entered into the dark thick black clouds. The power of the Rod of God created a force field around him to prevent any damage to his suit. The clouds then dissipated a little bit exposing what was in front of Sergeant Waggit. With looking left and right, Sergeant Waggit could see nothing but water. Then up ahead on the right hand side was a dock within the water. Sergeant Waggit ran over to the dock and walked onto it. He noticed a sign on the dock that said,

"Dead Soul Sea". Sergeant Waggit thought about it for a moment and had no idea if this was a trick or a trap. Then, Sergeant Waggit remembered that along his way he had found some gems that looked very valuable. He took out the gems and tossed them into the sea. Within a few moments, a boat arrived at the dock with a demon-like skeleton structure in a cloak guiding it. The skeleton looked at Sergeant Waggit and said, "Do you wish to cross?" Without any hesitation Sergeant Waggit quickly agreed to the skeleton with saying, "Yes." The skeleton then moved the boat into position to where it is docked with the dock. Sergeant Waggit then climbed aboard the boat. The skeleton then pushed the ore upon the boat to make it move away from the dock and head down the sea.

Sergeant Waggit looked at the skeleton and asked him, "So, what are you?" The skeleton then replied with turning its head towards Sergeant Waggit, "I am the ferryman of the dead soul sea." Sergeant Waggit then asked, "Where are you taking me?" The ferryman replied with a smile, "You are crossing the sea to a land known as the lair of Hades." Sergeant Waggit saw a bench upon the boat and sat down on it. After a long ride across the dead soul sea, the boat came upon another dock. The ferryman adjusted the order to allow the boat to dock with the dock. The ferryman looked right at Sergeant Waggit and said, "I will wait here for your return." Sergeant Waggit was confused as the ferryman said that he would wait there when he knew that he may be continuing on his mission. Sergeant Waggit stepped off the boat onto the dock and began to walk down a path that could lead him to the lair of Hades. After walking for quite a distance, Sergeant Waggit came upon a gate within a trunk of a very large tree. The gate was locked and required a special key to open it. Using the Rod of God, Sergeant Waggit tried to use all the different powers to open the gate but had no success. He looked around to see if there was anything around the area that he could use to open the gate or if there was any other way around but clearly the gate made the pathway a dead end. Sergeant Waggit turned around from the gate and headed back down the pathway to where the dock was at the dead soul sea. Once arriving at the dock, Sergeant Waggit saw the boat sitting there as the ferryman promised him his word. Sergeant Waggit walked onto the dock and climbed on board the boat. The ferryman looked at Sergeant Waggit and said, "You could not enter the gate, could you." Sergeant Waggit then said, "How did you know?" The ferryman then replied by saying, "I'm the ferryman of the dead soul sea. I see everything including the lands within the area of the sea." The ferryman then paused for a moment and then asked a question, "Where would you like to go?" Sergeant Waggit responded by saying, "Take me somewhere that I can continue my journey." The ferryman adjusted the ore of the boat to head towards an unknown area within the sea. After traveling through the sea for almost an hour, the ferryman stopped the boat. Sergeant Waggit looked all around and noticed that the boat had stopped. He looked at the ferryman and said, "What...? What is it?" The ferryman looked at Sergeant Waggit and said, "There is something within the sea that is forbidden and brought here by Hades. Sergeant Waggit then said, "What exactly do you see that is forbidden within the sea?" The ferryman then said, "I see monster fish, monster whales, and tentacles of a beast that is astonishing in size." The ferryman then opened a box and took something out of it. The object was some form of attachment and threw it at Sergeant Waggit. The ferryman then said, "Here... You are going to need this." Sergeant Waggit caught the object that was thrown to him. He observed it and noticed that the object was an attachment to his heavy cannon rifle. The attachment gave the rifle's ability to have a grenade launcher attached to it. Sergeant Waggit looked at the ferryman and said, "Thanks man." The ferryman then responded to Sergeant Waggit by saying, "Now that you have a grenade launcher for your rifle, open the box that's next to you and you will be rewarded with rounds of ammunition for your grenade launcher." Sergeant Waggit reached over to the box that was next to him and pried it open with the Rod of God. Once the lid was off the box, Sergeant Waggit shuffled through the loose paper and debris that was within the box to find nothing more than a huge belt of grenades that were designed for the grenade launcher. He put the belt around his waist and took out a grenade from the belt to load the grenade launcher.

Once Sergeant Waggit was ready for combat, a bunch of man-eating or flesh-eating fish began to jump out of the water over the boat and land back in the water on the other side of the boat. Sergeant Waggit saw the fish were not attacking him just yet but getting very close. He took out his Rod of God and got ready as the fish continued to fly over the boat. He used the rod as a large stick to bat away the fish when they got too close to him. One fish decided that it wanted to attack the rod and was larger than the other ones. The fish literally bit on the end of the rod and took it out of Sergeant Waggit's hands. The fish then fell onto the deck of the boat flopping around with the rod stuck in his mouth. Sergeant Waggit tried to activate the rod but could not reach the trigger that would allow him to put his hand on there as the fish mouth was over the trigger. Sergeant Waggit took out his heavy cannon rifle, aimed at the fish on the deck, and fired his first grenade from the grenade launcher. The grenade from the grenade launcher blew into the fish's mouth. The fish swallowed the grenade seconds before it was to go off. Sergeant Waggit picked up the rod and was swinging around with the fish still attached to it. Then the fish exploded as the grenade detonated within the fish's belly sending fish cuts all over the boat and all over Sergeant Waggit's suit. More fish continued to jump over the boat and Sergeant Waggit continued to fight them off until the fish stopped jumping. All of a sudden there were bursts of water blasting out of the surface of the ocean next to the boat. Sergeant Waggit yelled out, "What the fuck is that!!?" The ferryman looked at Sergeant Waggit and said, "That is the whales that are also man eaters or flesh eaters." Sergeant Waggit chuckled for a moment and then said, "Man eating whales. That is a new one." The whales then rotated their bodies enough to cause their blowhole to be faced towards the boat. one by one each whale blue it's water out of its blowhole directly towards Sergeant Waggit. Using the Rod of God, Sergeant Waggit was able to shield himself from the deadly blows that the whales were pumping out. After a short period of time from the deadly blows and hoping that his rod would continue to keep him safe, the whales stopped and vanished the area as if something else was there. Sergeant Waggit looked at the ferryman and said, "So, what now?" The water around the boat began to rumble as something was coming up towards the surface. The ferryman turned his head and looked right at the water that was bubbling within the depths of the sea and saw a large tentacle. He then turned to Sergeant Waggit and said, "Be prepared for a massive attack. It's the kraken." Sergeant Waggit then yelled out, "Oh shit!! The kraken is fuck'n real!!"

Blasting out of the water came a tentacle that was so large that it could literally cover the mid section of the boat. The tentacle stood almost one-hundred feet in the air sticking out of the sea. Then the tentacle began to curve in the air and come back down into the waters falling towards the boat. Sergeant Waggit used all of his weapons to attack the tentacle so it would not destroy the boat. After a series of blows within each weapon, the tentacle then lifted off through the water and went back down in the depths of the sea. Then on the other side of the boat approached another tentacle that was slightly a little bigger than the other one. Again, Sergeant Waggit used his weapons to attack this tentacle and prevented it from touching the boat. After a tremendous amount of rounds were spent from every weapon that he had, Sergeant Waggit watched the tentacle fall back into the sea below the ship. After a few moments it seemed like there was nothing else there but then Waters rumbled all around the boat in every direction. Then a huge tentacle that was about ten times the size of the boat came blasting out of the sea. Sergeant Waggit looked at this gigantic tentacle and then looked at the ferryman and yelled, "What the fuck am I supposed to do now!!? The ferryman looked at Sergeant Waggit and said, "Now, it is time for you to use the Rod of God." Sergeant Waggit then said to the ferryman, "Okay, I will get that out and be... wait, how do you know the name of the rod that I have?" The ferryman responded by saying, "Like I said, I can see everything." Sergeant Waggit pointed the rod towards the gigantic tentacle and began to use the power against it. at first it didn't seem like the power was going anywhere with this tentacle as all it was doing was just tickling it. The gigantic tentacle then started to curve and fall down towards the boat as it was going to land on top of Sergeant Waggit and the ferryman. Using the power with all his might and hoping that he could win with his strength within, Sergeant Waggit kneeled down holding the rod high up above his head near the tentacle as it was getting closer to the boat. The gigantic tentacle kept coming down closer and closer towards the boat causing Sergeant Waggit to lower his rod. It got to the point where Sergeant Waggit had to lay on the deck of the boat with the rod upon his chest holding it with a firm grip like if he was holding on to a rifle. When the gigantic tentacle was one foot above Sergeant Waggit and began destroying part of the boat as it crumbled the captain's deck to pieces, the Rod of God activated all of the stones that were within it and also channeled a power from Sergeant Waggit's chest causing the rod to glow extremely bright. Then all of a sudden a burst of energy from the rod blasted through the tentacle similar to an atom bomb smashing on the ground causing a mushroom cloud. The gigantic tentacle exploded into big chunks that splattered everywhere and the tail of the tentacle fell onto the deck of the boat. The other half of the tentacle that was destroyed went back into the sea below the boat. as the tentacle was going into the sea a tremendous amount of screaming noise from a creature below sounded as it was wounded. The bubbling of the water that was all around the ship ceased and the waters became calm once again. The tentacle tail that was sitting on the deck of the boat was curled up at the end. Sergeant Waggit walked over to the curl and used the Rod of God as a pry bar to unroll it. The curled tip within the tentacle end unrolled onto the deck of the ship. Within one of the suction cups of the tentacle was a glowing object. Sergeant Waggit said out loud, "Could it be!" He then took out his glove that was within his pouch and put it on his right hand. Sergeant Waggit then reached down and picked up the glowing object. He noticed that it was a stone of some sort but had no idea if it was when he was looking for or not. Sergeant Waggit placed the stone right above the Rod of God and the stone snapped into one of the slots and locked into place. the wrong thing began to change color once again and also change the shape a little bit to look more like a large staff. The stone that was collected was red in color and had some form of liquid flowing inside it. Sergeant Waggit used his computer system to analyze the stone that was just attached to the rod. The computer system recognized what the stone was and said, "The stone that was just recovered is known as the core stone." Sergeant Waggit was happy to see that he was still alive and that yet he found another stone. He asked the ferryman if he could continue his journey on where he needed to go. The ferryman agreed and began sailing his ship across the dead soul sea to the unknown that will lead Sergeant Waggit to his next area for discovery.

Traveling across the dead soul sea and heading towards the unknown, Sergeant Waggit was intrigued by his new findings and still stunned by the fact that he actually fought a kraken. Sergeant Waggit turned to look at the ferryman to see what he was up to. To his site, Sergeant Waggit watched the ferryman eat the tentacle that was lying on the deck of the boat. After a short period of time traveling across the sea, the ferryman started to drift the boat. Within the thick cloud that the boat was drifting through, a dock appeared that would allow the boat to approach it. Once the boat came to a stop at the new dock, Sergeant Waggit took all his gear and stepped off the boat onto the dock. Sergeant Waggit waved goodbye to the ferryman and yelled out, "Thanks for the ride!!" the ferryman nodded in agreement and turned the boat towards the sea and it headed off into the dark thick clouds vanishing out of sight.

CHAPTER FOURTEEN

Ancient Pyramid of the Ruins

Sergeant Waggit turned around and began heading down the long dock that he was standing on. Stepping down onto a sandy path, Sergeant Waggit continued his journey to find more stones and artifacts that he could use along his way. After a long vigorous and treacherous walk throughout the lands of a hot desert, Sergeant Waggit stumbled across another pyramid. However, this pyramid was a little different from the other ones that he had come across before. The pyramid was very tall and structured in size but it looked like an outer shell that was attached to such a rock structured pyramid. The outer shell was made of metal of some sort and it had four different layers that were separated by a series of lights with lights underneath and in between glowed with a red and white tint. As Sergeant Waggit approached the pyramid, the outer skeleton structure began to move and open up as if whatever was controlling it wanted light from outside to shine inside the stone structured pyramid. With caution, Sergeant Waggit walked through the entryway, which indeed was massive in size to wear a transformer or a giant alien could physically fit through it. Within the visual of his sight, Sergeant Waggit could see nothing more than just an engine pyramid with artifacts and markings that he had never seen before. On the wall to his right there was a saying within the Egyptian language that stated, "Ancient Pyramid of the Ruins". Sergeant Waggit used his scanner to capture the language that was written on the wall and put it into his database for later use in case maybe he may need it. Then just right next to the location of the ancient script upon the wall was a little box inside the wall that was carved out. Sergeant Waggit reached out and grabbed the box. With a little tug the box slid right out of the wall and there was nothing that happened afterwards. Sergeant Waggit was afraid that there would be some spell or some salt attack that would blast him as he took out the box from the wall but however that never happened. Sergeant Waggit stored the box in his travel pouch that he had for later use as he may need it somewhere within the pyramid.

Walking through the pyramid, Sergeant Waggit took many cautious steps to include looking around corners and having his weapons at the ready. One of the rooms within the pyramid had a brick wall door that was slightly open. Sergeant Waggit approached the door and heard a sound on the other side. The sound sounded like some sort of creature that was crunching on something and biting down on the bones or some form of crackling debris. By pulling onto the door and pushing it back and forth until it broke free, Sergeant Waggit was able to search the room to figure out where the noise was coming from. To his surprise, Sergeant Waggit was able to see a strange creature that looked human in shape but yet it had a mask upon its head. The mask looked bionic with some type of power source that allowed it to look real and feel real. The body that was structured around the mask was human with a strong sense of vibes and a six pack applied to the abs area indicating that the creature was physically fit. Holding a long spear-like structure with a beam of blue at the end of the spear, the creature turned around and looked right at Sergeant Waggit. The mouth of the bionic mask was covered in blood as it was just chomping down on some creature within the unknown. Sergeant Waggit looked at the creature as if it was staring his soul up and down. He said with a calm and autonomous voice, "Who... who or what are you?" The alien creature with the mask began to say something that was not English or any other language that was heard of. Sergeant Waggit then said, "We, that's just fuck'n great. I run into a creature and try to talk to it but I can't even understand what it's saying." Sergeant Waggit approached the masked creature to get a better look. The creature then took its spear and activated it to where it was ready for an attack. Sergeant Waggit stopped within his tracks and then said out loud with an excited voice, "Oh I see! That's how you want to start off this conversation! Fine! Take your way then!" Sergeant Waggit pointed his rifle directly towards the creature and fired upon it. The bullets penetrated The Hive of the creature killing it instantly. Then the mask revealed itself by mechanically changing to expose the head of the creature. The creature was merely just a man and nothing more.

Sergeant Waggit thought to himself, "If that creature was a man, then I wonder what language he was speaking as it's something that's not within my database and also something I've never heard of at all. In fact, I wonder if this man is actually a real man or if it's a machine like the Terminator kind of thing or if it's simply just some form of super being but with similar organs to a humanoid structure." With high intentions of not knowing what the creature was, Sergeant Waggit decided to perform an autopsy on the creature to see for himself. After using a bonsai and ripping open the rib cage to the creature, he noticed that there was nothing different within the creature than what was actually within himself. The creature indeed was human but might have been under a spell or something due to the mask that it was wearing. He also thought that the fact that the language could be coming from the mask and not from the human itself. He also did think that the human could possibly speak some language that he probably knows. Sergeant Waggit cleaned himself up and then left the alien creature to stay where it was. He then however picked up the mask and began to analyze it for anything that he can use. Within the head of the mask, Sergeant Waggit found a voice oscillator which would allow someone to alter their voice. With a few wires from his battery system on his arm, Sergeant Waggit was able to power up the voice oscillator. Sergeant Waggit then said something into the voice oscillator to see if it would change his voice or not. His voice on the other end came out similar to what the creature was saying. Sergeant Waggit then thought to himself out loud, "Well, this just may come in handy in case I run into another one of these sons of bitches." Sergeant Waggit attached the voice oscillator to his arm and had it be able to activate based on his thoughts and input from his computer system.

Sergeant Waggit continued his search through this ancient pyramid looking for what he needed along his path. In another room, Sergeant Waggit found a crate that was there glowing as if something very important was sitting inside it. Using the Rod of God, Sergeant Waggit smashed open the crate and revealed the item that was inside it. At the bottom of the crate there was a boomerang that had the same symbols and structure that was within the mask of the creature that he took down. Sergeant Waggit picked up the boomerang and attached it to the side of his utility belt. He then said to himself, "This boomerang looks very unique and cool at the same time and I hope that it can perform just as good as it looks." Sergeant Waggit heard another noise that was coming from the next room over. He stopped to look around to see if anyone was around him but there was nothing within his sight. Sergeant Waggit then secretly exited the room and headed over to the room that was next door. With high caution and high alert, Sergeant Waggit opened the door and saw another strange cybernetic creature standing there with the mask on. This time he was prepared and had this device that could alter his voice to understand what this creature was saying. The creature looked right at Sergeant Waggit and said something within its own language. The voice oscillator that was attached to Sergeant Waggit's arm did not respond to the creature's voice. Sergeant Waggit thought to himself, "Son of a bitch. I forgot to alter the voice oscillator to accept an incoming message." So instead he decided to say something which the voice oscillator would translate for him. Sergeant Waggit said out loud staring at the creature, "You look like a bionic bird that shit on himself and a feather that was shoved up your ass so damn far that you can feel it tickle your insides. if you understand what I just said scratch your balls for me so I know that I've made my point." The creature looked at Sergeant Waggit with its head side to side indicating that it was either understanding what he was saying or was intrigued by the type of tone that he was talking. Then the creature reached down and began to actually reach for his testicle location. Sergeant Waggit then said to himself out loud not knowing that the translator was still on, "Wow, that fuck'n worked. I got this bitch by his balls. He's my bitch now. He can do anything for me including kill his own kind." The creature heard everything that Sergeant Waggit had said and knew exactly what he was talking about. The creature then activated his spear and pointed directly at Sergeant Waggit. With noticing that the weapon was facing towards him, Sergeant Waggit I said out loud with the translator still on, "Really, you had to go there huh." Then Sergeant Waggit pointed his rifle towards the creature and let him up with multiple bullets killing the creature instantly. You then put his weapon away and begin to walk past the creature but then he stopped. Sergeant Waggit thought to himself, "Maybe I should fix the voice oscillator so that when the creature talks I can understand what it's saying." Sergeant Waggit examined the creature that was on the ground and looked at the mask on this particular one as it was a little different. He noticed that there was something within the ears of the head. Sergeant Waggit ripped off the head to the creature's mask and used his tools to remove such objects from the ears. The peace inside the ears was a translator. Sergeant Waggit installed the translator into the speaker system within his suit. Then, he turned on the voice oscillator and said something quickly like, "Who are you." The voice oscillator transferred the voice into the alien structured voice and the translator transferred the voice back to English. Sergeant Waggit then said to himself out loud, "Now we are getting somewhere."

Once again in another room there was a noise as if someone was running or banging into stuff. Sergeant Waggit secured his gear and headed over to that room to investigate it. After opening the door to the room where the noise was coming from, Sergeant Waggit noticed another creature that had a slightly different mask and this creature was a different color too. The creature noticed Sergeant Waggit running into the room and pointed its weapon directly at him. The creature then yelled something out extremely fast and a vigorous type voice but with the language that was unknown. The voice translator altered the voice to say, "Stop at once! Don't come any closer!" Sergeant Waggit stopped as quickly as he could. The creature turns his head to the side a little bit and then back to straight as he was concerned by the fact that this person or thing heard him. Sergeant Waggit then said out loud to the creature with a very calm voice, "I am here not to harm you but to ask you questions of your kind as I am not familiar with your type." After a short period of time of staring back and forth, the creature disarmed its weapon and put it down to the side as if it was like a cane or staff. The creature then began to talk and the translator began to say, "Go ahead with your question." Sergeant Waggit then asked his question calmly, "Who are you and where do you come from?" The creature began to talk and the translator translated every word by saying, "We are the Gods of the hypergiant Scuti star. We come here to locate a stone that is a great wonder. We have been searching for this particular Stone which was taken from us a long time ago. A stone is known as the Avida Stone. The stone's power is what generates our kind from the density of the star's inner core and to put life within our mechanical masks." Sergeant Waggit thought about it for a moment and then said, Well, I'm looking for the stone too. Maybe if we work together we can find the lost stone." The creature then said, allowing the translator to translate the information, "That sounds like a plan. Let me take you to our leaders and let them decide if we need your help or not. In order for me to take you to our leaders, you need to first put away your weapon as you may be a threat." Sergeant Waggit shouldered his weapon and then followed the creature throughout the pyramid to an unknown area with caution.

The creature led Sergeant Waggit to an open area that had a chamber that looked as if it was Royal. There was a chair sitting in the middle of the room and on both sides of it were statues that were birds with giant horns that were symbols for some form of demonic race. Behind the chair were some stairs that led them to an unknown room that had a barrier wall within the tomb to shield whatever's behind it. As the creature and Sergeant Waggit approached the chair, the doors that were behind the chair within the tomb opened up showing other creatures that lurked within. Sergeant Waggit stared at the creatures and counted a total of three of them. It's all nothing but the same similarities of men dressed in some form of uniform but with a bionic mask they covered their entire upper half of their body. The bionic masks looked nothing more than like Minotaurs. On both sides of the middle Minotaur were two Minotaurs in silver color. The middle Minotaur was gold in color signifying that he was the leader. Sergeant Waggit wanted to approach these creatures and ask them for their help in finding the Avida Stone. Instead, it was merely nothing but a trap and Sergeant Waggit had no idea what was going to happen next. The creature that led him to this chamber used its weapon and struck Sergeant Waggit's legs from behind causing him to fall down onto his knees. The creature using his voice oscillator said out loud with the translator translating the message, "You will bow to him!" The three Minotaurs approached Sergeant Waggit. The Minotaur in the middle wearing the gold mask sat down into the chair while the other two Minotaurs stood beside the chair on either side of it. Sergeant Waggit found that it would be a good opportunity at that moment to attack the Minotaurs but chose not to; instead he wanted to listen to hear their message before he would be too late. The golden Minotaur looked at Sergeant Waggit and began to speak with the translator translating his message, "You are here to kill me and all of my men. I see all and everything within all walls. Two of my men are destroyed and one of them is gutted. You have taken valuable assets of their armor and used it to translate our language to you. For this you will die and you will not prevail within the walls of my chambers." Sergeant Waggit took out his Rod of God and began to strike down the soldier that led him to the three Minotaurs. Then he turned around and began to attack both the right and left silver Minotaurs. The golden Minotaur stood up off of his chair, wearing a cape behind him made out of wool from an animal. He dropped the cape onto the chair and said, "You can try but you will never win." The golden Minotaur took out a weapon that came out of nowhere and began to use it against Sergeant Waggit. Using the Rod of God, Sergeant Waggit shot out multiple different types of combinations trying to eliminate the threat of the golden Minotaur. Bursts of rounds flew in energy molds across the room trying to hit the armor within the center of Sergeant Waggit. As the rounds came near, Sergeant Waggit dodged them as if he was in a slow motion movie similar to the movie, "Matrix". The golden Minotaur continued to fight and came up with more destructive combinations that made it very difficult for Sergeant Waggit to keep on attacking and blocking. Some of the rounds of energy came in contact with Sergeant Waggit's shoulders and legs piercing them making him bleed and falling to the ground.

Without showing any mercy, Sergeant Waggit slowly came back up under his feet to face this enemy. The golden Minotaur ran over to him as quickly as he could and struck his chest, throwing Sergeant Waggit up against the walls smacking his back against it and then falling down onto his hands and knees. Sergeant Waggit could not bear the pain anymore that this creature is causing on him. As Sergeant Waggit stood up again he reached back and grabbed the Rod of God and held it firmly in front of him. The golden Minotaur ran across the floor as fast as it could trying to make a massive attack against Sergeant Waggit. Withholding the Rod of God with all his might, Sergeant Waggit picked up the rod with both hands and then slammed it down on the ground and yelled out, "The almighty! I bargain for your power! Face this enemy and a soul you'll devour!" A blast came from the Rod of God and spread out all across the room in every direction from where Sergeant Waggit was standing. The golden Minotaur flew across the room and smacked up against the wall and fell onto the ground. Then of course with the beast thinking that it was done got back up and began to charge Sergeant Waggit. As the golden Minotaur approached the Rod of God, the rod began to glow white with a tint of blue. The golden Minotaur reached out and grabbed the rod. As his hands became firm on the rod, a mysterious power channeled through the rod into the Minotaur causing it to suffer and feed on light and fear at the same time. After a short period of time, the golden Minotaur released its grip and fell to the ground. It's mask came undone and revealed who he really was. The face upon the enemy that was fighting Sergeant Waggit was nothing more than a lost soldier from Earth during the Roman Era. Sergeant Waggit felt bad that he had fought a man but he knew that he had been stopped as the man was going to kill him. Sergeant Waggit opened up his utility pouch that he was carrying around his waist and took out a dressing kit. He applied the kid to the wounds upon his shoulder and leg to prevent himself from bleeding anymore. Sergeant Waggit thought to himself out loud, "I... I thought that I was indestructible. But now I know I'm not. My powers are leaving me and my suit is becoming more vulnerable everyday. Now I know what needs to be done. I need to find the rest of the stones so that I can be immortal and set balance to the universe."

Sergeant Waggit rested within the chamber that he defeated the minotaurs sitting in the leader's chair. After a few days of resting allowing the wounds to heal, Sergeant Waggit packed up all of his gear and secured his weapons. He got up and began to head out of the chamber. Just as Sergeant Waggit was about to exit the chamber he heard a loud clunk noise and then turned around. He noticed that the chair he was sitting in was starting to sink into the ground as if it was being pulled into the ground by a mechanical device. After the chair disappeared, a chest came up from the ground in the place where the chair was. Sergeant Waggit said to himself out loud, "Could it be? Could have I found the next Stone?" Sergeant Waggit then waddled over to the chest and pried it open the best he could. As the chest opened up, Sergeant Waggit's eyes gleamed as he saw glow within the chest base. On top of the glow there was a cloth of some sort covering it. With high hopes and excitement within his heart, Sergeant Waggit reached in and removed the cloth from the chest. His excitement went from a ten to a zero instantly when he knew that there was no stone. However, there was something in the chest that he would be able to use along his way. Sergeant Waggit reached inside the chest and removed the artifact that was sitting in it. The glowing artifact was a diamond and there was a handle attached to it. The diamond was in the shape of a hammerhead. Sergeant Waggit thought to himself, "This is cool. I will have to test this new weapon out on the next enemy that I see. Since the head of this weapon is diamond, it should be extremely strong and should be able to cut through anything that comes in contact with it. It's a bummer that I did not get a stone, however, this new weapon makes up for it. All I need now is a fuck'n bottle of champagne to celebrate my victory." Sergeant Waggit secured the new weapon to the side of his utility belt and then stepped out of the chamber that he was in. He followed a pathway through the pyramid until he saw daylight which was a slight little hole in the wall. Sergeant Waggit reached back to get his grenade launcher and then he thought about it for a second and decided to reach for the new hammer. With a single blow, the hammer smashed through the wall, crumbling it down exposing the outside light onto Sergeant Waggit's face. Sergeant Waggit stepped outside and began to head down a path just beyond the pyramid.

CHAPTER FIFTEEN

Court Yard of Deception

It was a long hot walk along the pathway leaving the pyramid in the past. Sergeant Waggit looked for more signs of things that he could search through to locate any other stone or any other artifact that can help them along his way. After the sun was getting ready to set in the horizon ahead, Sergeant Waggit noticed a sign that was up ahead along the path. The sign read, "To the right is the Pyramid of the Ruins and to the left is the Courtyard of Deception." Sergeant Waggit said to himself out loud, "Well, I guess I'm heading towards the Courtyard of Deception." You then continue this path along the way looking for anything that he could use. Then up ahead was a glowy substance underneath the pathway and the pathway had a very long bridge. When Sergeant Waggit approached the bridge he stopped in his tracks and looked at the glowy substance. At first he thought it was water and then he realized it was not. Sergeant Waggit said out loud with an excited voice, "That shit down there is lava!" Looking ahead along the pathway across the bridge, Sergeant Waggit noticed that the lava was spewing up all over the place and fleeing from one side to the other side of the bridge. Sergeant Waggit thought to himself, "Well, how hard can it be? I went through a mind that had a bunch of lava or magma underneath the tracks and I survived."

Sergeant Waggit walked onto the bridge and began to cross the enormous long bridge with magma spewing up from depths below. He had to dodge multiple blobs of magma that would fly from the right side to the left side and then also from the left side to the right side. It was as if the magma was purposely trying to attack Sergeant Waggit. Even though the bridge was made out of wood with concrete barriers underneath it and steel beneath that, there were holes within the wooden deck of the bridge. Sometimes the magma would shoot up through the holes and then come straight back down. Sergeant Waggit noticed a bunch of obstacles that were blocking his way but there were a lot of holes as well. With perfect timing in between magma spewing up and down through the holes, Sergeant Waggit carefully jumped over each hole trying not to get hit as he would not know if his suit could handle the extreme temperatures of the molten rock. After passing over five different holes and merely almost getting clipped by one of the blobs floating up through a hole, Sergeant Waggit safely made it across that section of the bridge. To make it even more difficult, there were more holes to the number of twelve or more with magma spewing through them and dead zombie soldiers with swords standing around the holes waiting for his arrival. Sergeant Waggit took out his missile launcher and began to shoot each of the soldiers one at a time. The soldiers were not going to give up that easy. Each one of them jumped and dodged the round coming at it. Sergeant Waggit said to himself with great anger and his voice, "Alright you sons of bitches, you shall feel the power of my hammer!" Sergeant Waggit ran up to the first dead zombie soldier that was holding a sword and took out his diamond hammer. With one big blow, Sergeant Waggit jumped in the air dodging the soldiers blade and smashing his hammer directly on top of the soldier's head destroying it to pieces. Then he continued jumping over each hole one at a time dodging the blobs of magma flying up into the air and attacking the other soldiers one by one until they were all dead. Sergeant Waggit safely made it past all the holes and all the soldiers lying there dead crumbled into pieces. He turned around to look to see if anything was still standing and saw that there was nothing there. With an amazing growling sensation along with his voice, Sergeant Waggit yelled out, "Aaahhh!! That's how you fuck'n do it!!"

Continuing to strive to cross the long bridge, Sergeant Waggit had to fight off more dead zombie soldiers and jump over even more obstacles. Then, while running across the bridge with great speed, Sergeant Waggit came to a halt screeching his feet causing his boots to make a sound similar to chalk rubbing against a chalkboard. Part of the bridge in front of Sergeant Waggit was broken out with a long distance across with no way to get over. Sergeant Waggit thought about it for a moment and then took out the Rod of God. He sent the power of it to perform the ice and was able to spread eyes all the way across but noticed that the magma would melt it down quickly. So instead, he decided to dump ice into giant blocks onto the magma so it would melt but allow him to climb onto the blocks and continue making more blocks until you reach the other side of the bridge. What Sergeant Waggit didn't know is that the blocks of ice would melt rather quicker than he thought. When he reached the last block of ice and was about to jump onto the edge of the bridge, the ice block melted all the way down as he jumped up in the air. The only thing that kept him from falling into the magma below was the Rod of God that he was holding got caught on the edge of the bridge. Sergeant Waggit used all his might and upper strength to climb up the rod without the rod falling and without him falling until he was able to be safe on top of the bridge. After he was safely resting on top of the bridge, Sergeant Waggit noticed that the Rod of God was still hanging off the edge. He reached over to pick up the rod but right when he did so a dead zombie soldier appeared stepping over him and knocking the rod over the edge. Sergeant Waggit yelled out with fear and his face, "Nooooooo!" He took out his rocket launcher and stuck it to the chest of the dead zombie soldier and pulled the trigger. Sergeant Waggit yelled out, "Eat this!!" The rocket propelled out of the launcher and when it came in contact with the soldier, the round exploded shearing the soldier to pieces with guts flying everywhere. Sergeant Waggit looked over the edge with tears coming out from his eyes as he knew he had lost everything. After wiping the tears away on getting a better glimpse of the magma below, Sergeant Waggit noticed that the Rod of God was just laying on top of the magma with a glow shining just beneath it. Sergeant Waggit said to himself out loud, "Only if I could create an ice block that rod would come back to me." He then remembered that he had the spell book with him. Sergeant Waggit took out the spell book and opened it to the page that would allow him to create ice. He read the spell out loud and this is what it said, "Water drop and form, create ice under the norm, make a block that I could see, raise the rod unto me." For a moment nothing happened then out of the blue with a tear dropping from Sergeant Waggit's face, a block of ice formed underneath the rod pushing the rod all the way up to the level edge of the bridge. Sergeant Waggit reached out and grabbed the Rod of God. He secured it and then put the spell book back away. Sergeant Waggit then said to himself, "I hope I don't have to do that again." He then got up and continued running across the bridge in the search for another stone and other elements of surprise that could help him along the way.

As the bridge was still being long by the day with Sergeant Waggit continuing to run along it, up ahead was a mountain with magma flowing down from it as the belly of its mouth was spewing magma from the top. The bridge was broken up to many different bridges elapsed over each other going up the mountain. Sergeant Waggit had to jump onto the other bridges and some of the bridges he had to find some way to climb up them. Once reaching the very top bridge at the top of the mountain, Sergeant Waggit again came to a screeching halt as the bridge ended right at the belly of the mouth of the volcano mountain. He yelled out, "What the fuck?! What the hell am I supposed to do now?! What am I supposed to just jump into the lava below?!" Sergeant Waggit thought about it for a moment and then got a brilliant idea. He decided to use the Rod of God to produce land mass and cause it to collapse on each other. Withholding the rod over the volcano he activated the power to create the landmass and allow the mountain to collapse on itself. As the landmass was falling and the mountain was collapsing, the magma stopped flowing and began to harden. Once everything seemed like it was normal and ended to where Sergeant Waggit could continue his adventure, the most unspeakable thing happened. A statue that represented the king of the demons of the underworld came plowing through the magma on top of the mountain. Sergeant Waggit said to himself, "You have got to be shitting me." The statue that appeared through the magma was the statue of Pazuzu. Pazuzu was a demonic god who was very powerful that could summon the winds to destroy anything. Sergeant Waggit looked at the statue and said, "Well, it's just a statue what horn could it do." The Pazuzu statue cast out onto Sergeant Waggit possessing his soul. Sergeant Waggit's eyes began to glow red signifying that the spirit of the Pazuzu was embedded within his soul. The spirit of the Pazuzu was trying to make Sergeant Waggit kill himself by leaping off the bridge and plunging into the hardened molten rock below that would break and cause him to melt to eternity. Sergeant Waggit stepped off the bridge and fell all the way towards the magma. Just inches before touching the magma, Sergeant Waggit stopped and hovered above it. The statue of the Pazuzu turned its head down to see what was happening. The Rod of God that was attached to the back side of Sergeant Waggit's armor was glowing blue and white. Sergeant Waggit looked around and saw that he was not dead nor was he falling anymore and floating in mid-air. He looked down between his legs and saw the glow once again and knew that it was coming from the rod. He reached behind him and took out the Rod of God and held it in his hands with a firm grip. Sergeant Waggit was excited for the fact that he did not die and now he has the full potential power for what is unknown to his understanding about the rod. Sergeant Waggit yelled out, "Yes, baby yes!" He then could turn the rod left or right and cause himself to float in those directions with a quickness. This gave the illusion that Sergeant Waggit was actually flying. Sergeant Waggit looked at the statue and yelled out, "Ha, ha! Now you're fucked!"

The Pazuzu statue began to show multiple cracks all within it with a cracking sound. Then within the very last second after the cracking sound had stopped, the Pazuzu statue exploded, throwing the rock everywhere and leaving exposed a red and yellow demon. The little demon that was on Sergeant Waggit's shoulder got scared and climbed into Sergeant Waggit's suit. Sergeant Waggit looked at the little demon into his suit and asked, "What is to be afraid of, little guy?" The little demon grunted and then tried to say something. It was saying, "Th... th..., the demon. The demon is my father. Save me. Save me from death." Sergeant Waggit zipped up his suit to secure the little demon inside. He then began to fight the Pazuzu demon. The Pazuzu demon began to swing it's arms at Sergeant Waggit. Then it lunged towards him with great speed. Sergeant Waggit rotated the rod so that he could dodge every blow that the demon produced. Once the demon was tired from making so many different attacks similar to a boxer being tired after throwing a bunch of punches, Sergeant Waggit used multiple counter attacks against the demon to weaken the demon's ability to survive. After multiple counterattacks and dodging multiple lunges from the demon, Sergeant Waggit was able to defeat the demon and make the demon fall to the ground. Sergeant Waggit thought that the demon was dead for sure but then it got back up and grew in size. The Pazuzu demon changed form to one of the soldiers that was on Sergeant Waggit's mind. With Sergeant Waggit staring at a soldier that he thought was already dead not knowing that the soldier was actually the demon, Sergeant Waggit approached the soldier to help him. The demon kept on egging Sergeant Waggit to follow his lead to the dark side of life and join him in the most impressive battle of all time. Sergeant Waggit could not resist the temptation that the demon was applying to his soul and wanted to move with him as he had a dark side to his past. However, the power that was raging through the rod gripped in his hands was not going to allow him to follow this demon to an eternal death. The power of the Rod of God opened up Sergeant Waggit's suit and released the little cute demon. The power made the little cute demon grow into an astronomical size. Then without any warning signs, the little cute demon that was giant reached down with its mouth and ate the Pazuzu demon. After gulping down the demon, the little cute demon which was very large belched very loud. Then the little cute demon that was very large shrunk back to his normal self and fell into Sergeant Waggit's left hand. The little cute demon looked at Sergeant Waggit and said, "I'm finally free." Then the little cute demon turned into a blue light and stretched to vanish with an existence.

The power from the rod of God lifted up Sergeant Waggit and took him to a courtyard where he could be safe from all evil. Up ahead of his location from the courtyard, Sergeant Waggit saw a giant tower creating a huge shadow across the lands. Without any hesitations, Sergeant Waggit packed up all his stuff and made sure that everything was secure. Then he began his journey through the courtyard towards this giant tower.

CHAPTER SIXTEEN

Tower of Terror

After crossing the courtyard and spending countless hours doing so, Sergeant Waggit reached the giant tower that was high enough to cover the entire courtyard if it was to fall over. The interesting thing about the tower wasn't really how tall it was or how big it was but rather its state where it is to be standing. The tower is merely floating off the ground and has four large chains holding it in place which are anchored to the ground. The tower looked as if it was made of rock or a mountain that was dug up from the surface below. The building had a metal structure that went around the rock then also rotated in a slow fashion manner. Alongside of the metal structure were attached long channels they looked like additional rooms with hallways leading to them. Above the metal structure was a giant ring that went around the entire rock that was stationary. On the Rock just above the giant ring was fiery windows indicating light coming from within. The top of the building had a beam like structure coming out of it along with a form of energy flowing from the bottom of the beam through the top of the beam. Sergeant Waggit examined this unique floating building rock structure to determine where is the entry point and how to access it. After thinking for a moment, he knew what the next step was. Sergeant Waggit needed to climb on the chains all the way to the big ring that was stationary. This was not going to be an easy task as the height was very high off the ground and one fall smooth could lead Sergeant Waggit to his death.

Sergeant Waggit quickly put away all of his weapons and secured everything to be very tight so they would not fall off his suit. Then, he reached out and grabbed onto the first chain on the left that was near him. Sergeant Waggit used upper body strength to pull them onto the chain and then wrapped his legs around it so he could begin climbing towards the building along the chain. As Sergeant Waggit was approaching the building while climbing the chain, he noticed that there was going to be some obstacles along his way. Parts of the chain had fire upon them while other parts of the chain had spikes and unknown liquids dripping off of it. To make things even more dramatic for the scenario scene that he is climbing, Sergeant Waggit saw zombie monkeys climbing down the chain with little swords in their hands. As the zombie monkeys came closer, Sergeant Waggit grabbed his newly acquired hammer that he had attached to his utility belt and smacked them to oblivion. Each zombie monkey would shatter their bones into pieces falling from the chain and plunging into the surface below. For when it came to him having to move away from the fire applied to the chain, Sergeant Waggit flipped himself over onto the top of the chain so that he could lunge across it with a quick jump. The first time that he did this, his right foot slid off the chain causing him to hang from there. While holding on for dear life, Sergeant Waggit swung back and forth and was able to throw his feet back over the chain so he was secured once again. Then Sergeant Waggit came across some large spikes that were applied on the chain. Very carefully, he used the hammer to slowly smack the spikes hoping that they would not break the chain. One by one each spike broke off falling off the chain and plunging into the crown below burying itself deep within the lands of the courtyard. Now that Sergeant Waggit was three quarters the way up the chain, he came across the liquid that was dripping off. The liquid was not just any liquid. Sergeant Waggit grabbed his heavy cannon rifle and held it far enough out so that the liquid would drip onto the barrel grip. The liquid started burning through the plastic covering of the barrel grip. Sergeant Waggit knew at that point that the liquid was molecularly acid. The acid was so powerful that it would melt through metal which also means it would melt right through his suit and could cause him to go into cardio rest or even die if the acid was to get in the wrong place.

The molecular acid was still dripping off the chain and Sergeant Waggit had to think of a plan to go around so he would not come in contact with the contaminated area. With a light bulb appearing above his head, Sergeant Waggit got a brilliant idea. He decided to take out a tube that had some water in it and splash the acid compound with it. of course the asan began to react to the water causing it to splatter in multiple different directions. Then Sergeant Waggit took out the Rod of God and pointed it towards the acid compound. He then activated the ice power and applied a large block of ice over the acid to freeze the area. Sergeant Waggit rolled himself over on the chain and climbed onto the ice block. He carefully crossed the ice block as the acid was melting the ice. As soon as Sergeant Waggit pulled himself off the ice block and back onto the chain, the ice block melted completely away exposing the acid once again. Sergeant Waggit was glad that he came up with the idea to freeze the acid as it was the only plan for him to cross that part of the chain without being infected. Now that Sergeant Waggit passed all the hazard zones within the chain, he continued to claim the chain until he reached the large ring.

Climbing up onto the big ring was quite a bit of a challenge. After standing on top of the big ring, Sergeant Waggit saw multiple entryways into an underground cavern that was within this floating building. He began to start with the clos-est opening and entering into the caverns that were within this giant rock. Searching for the next Stone and any artifacts was his most import-ant adventure along his way through the caverns. Sergeant Waggit had to face multiple dead soldiers and small demons that lurked at him while he was searching for his artifacts. Most of the soldiers were packing weapons and would fire at him or pick up stones and Chuck them towards him try-ing to knock him off his path. Sergeant Waggit dodged every round that he could even though he still came in contact with rounds that punctured through his suit. With more wounds to clean up, Sergeant Waggit was not going to give up that easy and found his inner anger that leashed out into a burst of madness energy. The little demons would claw at his suit trying to attack him and with not having the little cute demon with him any-more made it more difficult for Sergeant Waggit to eliminate the little demons. After a long vig-orous attack through the caverns, Sergeant Waggit found multiple chests that had lots of health kits and weapon replenishing rounds that he had spent destroying those monsters.

After clearing the base level throughout the caverns, Sergeant Waggit came out and saw that there were some ladders nearby. He climbed the ladders to where he could enter the upper level of the caverns. Once again, Sergeant Waggit searched more areas of the caverns within this floating city or known as a giant rock. He found a lot of other items that could help him along the way like a torch and he did locate a map that would disclose all of the rooms within these caverns. Once the middle grounds were cleared, Sergeant Waggit continued his way to locate any stones or anything that additionally could help him. As he neared the top of the mountain structure, there was a very large door that was red in color. Sergeant Waggit tried to open the door but noticed that it was locked. He thought to himself out loud, "There must be a key somewhere within these caverns." Sergeant Waggit headed back down through the caverns all the way down to the bottom where the ring was. Using the map, Sergeant Waggit was able to pinpoint a secret area that was actually blocked off by some rubble. Sergeant Waggit used his grenade launcher to destroy the rubble that was up against the secret area. The secret area was then exposed and opened up the channel That was just below the ring. Sergeant Waggit jumped down into the area below the lower ring and headed down a hallway that led him to an area that had a really long arm like a short narrow hallway. At the end of the long narrow hallway, Sergeant Waggit entered a very large room and saw a chest within it. He opened the chest and found a key but the key was not red. As he was holding the key up in the air, Sergeant Waggit noticed that the key was blue. He said to himself, "What the fuck. Well I guess somewhere here in this caverns is going to be a blue door and I must find it." Sergeant Waggit left the room that he was in and headed down the long narrow hallway. He ran all the way around the rotating ring that was below the stationary ring. On the other end there was another long hallway with some sort of door at the end. Getting very close to the door, Sergeant Waggit noticed that it was blue in color. Sergeant Waggit approached the door and took out the blue key that he had recently found. He inserted the key into the slot that was on the door and turned it. The key opened up the door and revealed a new room. the room was just as big as the other room that he was in and there was another chest that was in the middle of the room. Sergeant Waggit walked up to the chest and opened it. Inside the chest was another key. Sergeant Waggit took out the key and held it up in the air to see what color it was and discovered that it was red. He secured the key and then headed out of the room as quickly as he could and ran down the hallway. He literally tried to find her way back up into the stationary ring but it was having troubles. Then he discovered another secret area that had some rubble in front of it. Using his grenade launcher, Sergeant Waggit blasted the rubble to pieces exposing a ladder behind it. Sergeant Waggit grabbed the hold of the rails to the ladder and began to climb which led him to the upper ring. He then ran all the way up toward the red door. When Sergeant Waggit approached the door he took out the red key and inserted it into the slot. After turning the key, the door opened up showing a stairway that was going very high and far away. Sergeant Waggit climbed up the stairway to see where it led him. After a long climb, Sergeant Waggit ran into another set of doors that he was able to open. Once the doors swung open, Sergeant Waggit's gleamed very big as a golden room was exposed. In the middle of the golden room there was a very large chest. Quickly, Sergeant Waggit ran over to the chest and opened it. Inside the chest was this unique chain and nothing different. With a puzzle look on his face, Sergeant Waggit was trying to figure out what the chain was for. He thought to himself out loud, "This is a weird find. What the hell am I going to do with the chain? What am I going to choke an enemy to death, or hang them, or what?" Sergeant Waggit looked inside the chest and saw that there was a piece of torn paper in there. He removed the paper and there was a drawing on it. The drawing was a hammer with a chain attached to it. Sergeant Waggit removed his hammer from his utility belt and looked at it. On the end of the handle there was a chain link that was open. Sergeant Waggit took the chain that he just acquired and attached it to the open link. Once the chain was in place the link closed on its own securing the chain to the hammer. Sergeant Waggit then picked up the hammer and threw it out as far as he could allowing the chain to slip through his hand. Near the very end of the chain he gripped his hand as hard as he could stopping the hammer in midair. Sergeant Waggit began to start to swing the hammer around as quickly as he could. The hammer created an unusual whisk of air like a cyclone being drawn from all areas within the room. Once he was done swinging the hammer around, Sergeant Waggit tugged on the chain to make the hammer fling back to his hand. He secured the hammer with the chain to his utility belt. Sergeant Waggit's face gleamed with gratitude as he was happy to see an upgrade to another weapon.

After securing the weapon to his utility belt, Sergeant Waggit noticed a lever that was in the middle of the room near the chest. He decided to walk over there and pull on this lever to see what would happen. After the lever was moved from one location to another, a doorway was exposed off to the side within the room he was residing in. Sergeant Waggit then headed towards this open doorway and saw that there was a spiral staircase. He headed up towards whatever was above the spiral staircase. At the end of the spiral staircase there was an entryway to another room. Inside this other room there were mechanical parts all over the place. The parents look like robotic pieces to machinery, like arms and legs of some sort of creature. Sergeant Waggit searched the room for anything he could use and then decided that he would pick up one of the robotic arms that were laying on the ground. When touching the robotic arm, the room began to shake as if there was a tremor happening within the ground. then one of the walls broke down and a giant scorpion came flying through the wall in a robotic form. Sergeant Waggit looked at this indigenous creature and yelled out, "What the fuck!! Are you fuck'n kidding me!! It could have been anything... any thing in the world but instead it had to be a fuck'n scorpion. And a robotic one too!!" Sergeant Waggit faced this massive creature with a giant tail with a laser cannon attached to it and the pinchers were merely nothing but barrels from a warthog aircraft. Each of the guns applied to the arms had seven barrels each with tipless explosive rounds. Sergeant Waggit did whatever it took to fight this creature and not die from the rounds hitting him. He ran and jumped over the barrels as they were spinning and shooting bullets in every direction. Hey dodged the blast of beans that kept coming from the tail. Sergeant Waggit used every weapon that he had to destroy this creature. The only thing that was left for him to use was the Rod of God and the diamond hammer. Sergeant Waggit used the power of the Rod of God to try to destroy this creature but it wasn't enough. He merely just stunned it and allowed it to lay on the ground with stars over its head indicating that it was injured or knocked out. After multiple attempts trying to destroy the creature, Sergeant Waggit was fed up with the creature not dying. He grabbed the diamond hammer and began to spin it around as quick as he could holding onto the chain. The hammer slammed into the robotic scorpion extremely hard. The robotics scorpion flew across the room slamming up against the wall laying on its side with its belly exposed. With extreme amounts of anger coming from Sergeant Waggit's face and mouth similar to what Liu Kang did during the final battle in the movie, "Mortal Kombat", he swung the hammer around as fast as he could around and plowed it into the belly of the beast. The hammer crushed the belly of the robotic scorpion exposing everything that was inside it, killing it instantly. Once the robotics scorpion stopped moving and opened up the belly a little bit more, a glowing object appeared next to one of the internal organs. Sergeant Waggit climbed up on top of the scorpion's belly and reached in to take out this glowing object. The glowing object was a stone. As the stone began to burn Sergeant Waggit's and as he was holding it, he quickly reached into his pouch and removed his glove and put it on the other hand. Similar to a hot potato in your hand, Sergeant Waggit tossed the stone into the hand with the glove on. He took out the Rod of God and put the stone near it. The stone found its place within the rod and locked into the groove that was originally cut into it. A new power was applied to the rod with a lightning bolt going around it. The computer system within Sergeant Waggit's suit scanned the newly acquired stone and broadcast a message for Sergeant Waggit to hear. The message said, "The stone that was just acquired is known as the Avida Stone." Sergeant Waggit said to himself out loud, "I'm glad to find the Avida Stone. Now I only have one more Stone to go and then I could return to the Andromeda Galaxy."

Sergeant Waggit headed out of the room and down the staircase towards the stationary ring. He found a cloth on a table and used it as a hand glider to glide down from the floating structure to a pathway just on the other side of a chain attached to the ground. As Sergeant Waggit headed down a path towards a hill that was nearby, the ground gave out, sending him to a dungeon that was under the surface.

CHAPTER SEVENTEEN

Shaft's Untold Truth

The fall was treacherous and seemed like it took forever. Sergeant Waggit slammed onto the ground and he heard a loud crack. At first he thought that he had broken a leg or something because the leg is mechanical and he would not even know whether he broke it or not because he wouldn't feel the impact. For his sake, Sergeant Waggit's leg was not broken but rather a large stick underneath it was. Sergeant Waggit stood up and looked around to see exactly where he was. To his knowledge, Sergeant Waggit knew that he was in some underground chamber or something as it was similar to another location that he had gone to on Earth a long time ago. Underneath the ground was a dungeon used to keep slaves within the walls from the fearless leader of Hades. Being dark down inside the dungeon, Sergeant Waggit took the torch that he had and lit it up with his Rod of God so that he could see what the walls and the hallways looked like. The walls were made of stone with pillars holding up the roof above along with the ground also being stoned but more of a path type stone rather than bricks. The walls also had green moss grown all over them along with the floor indicating that there had been water within the dungeon walls for quite some time. By some of the pillars there were wooden barrels that look like wine barrels. Sergeant Waggit walked over to a barrel and tried to examine it. He couldn't break it open with his bear hands so instead he took out his diamond hammer and slammed it directly on top of the barrel. The barrel splintered all over the place as it was destroyed when the hammer came into contact with it. Inside the barrel was a medical kit that he could use along his way in case something was to surprise him.

Sergeant Waggit walked through the dungeon in search of other artifacts and to see the whereabouts of the last location of the last stone. Along the way he saw a room that was off to the right that was open. Sergeant Waggit walked into the room and noticed there were a couple shelves against the walls. Looking at the shelves there were multiple artifacts on top of each shelf. There was a small box that had a key in it. On another shelf there was a set of flippers that would attach to Sergeant Waggit's feet. On the other shelf on the other wall had multiple boxes of rounds of ammunition that he could use to replenish what was spent in the last firefight. After securing all the artifacts and supplies, Sergeant Waggit left the room and continued down the dungeon to see where it was going to lead him. As he continued to walk he ran into an open room where there were twelve statues lined up in a row on the left side. Sergeant Waggit examined each statue one at a time. He noticed a resemblance that each statue was of a woman. The statues were in different positions showing the woman either with their hands to her side, to her torso, to holding something in her hand like an apple or a vase. The statues all had horns applied to the top of them along with a wardrobe dress of amazing style. Each statue was in the color of gray and green with a tint of gold for the face and arms. There was moss all over the statues indicating water had been through this known area causing a growth upon them. The two statues that were right in the middle were slightly different from the others. Of the statues that were in the middle, the statute on the right was the same woman but wearing a cloak type cape. The statue that was on the left from the middle was wearing armor applied to the waist and the legs indicating that the woman might have been a knight of some sort. Sergeant Waggit could not get a grass of what the woman was or what her story is behind all of these statues, however, by examining each statue you knew that the woman was truly in love with someone and showed her affections and multiple different ways but yet defended her land as Royal.

After he was done examining all the statues and trying to figure out the resemblance between all of them, Sergeant Waggit began to walk past them into the next room. When entering the next room, there were multiple cages that had bones applied to them indicating the people were trapped there as prisoners for a very long time. Sergeant Waggit sifted through the bones seeing if they left anything behind that could be useful. One of the bones had a little package underneath it. Sergeant Waggit picked up the package and opened it to see what it was. Inside the package was a little card that was written in stone. The message on the card said, "Beware of who lurks within these walls as they are not who you think they are. And when I mean they I mean only one being. This being is the female species of all love that was lost to the dungeons of below. Men suffer day in and day out for the lack of love that she gave them. She gave birth to multiple children for all the men that were locked up within the bars and buried them when they were suffering. Knowing that one day she'll return as dark as it could be, the love will be shed upon these bars releasing everyone." Sergeant Waggit tried to understand the message to figure out what it was giving him. He stored away the card into his pouch on his utility belt. Sergeant Waggit turned towards a doorway that was at the end of the open room and began heading in that direction. The fire that was lit on the torches that were like candles on the walls began to move in such a direction as if there was a draft in the open room. Sergeant Waggit stopped in his tracks as he saw a shadow hovering over his location. He slowly turned around to see what was casting such a shadow. Once Sergeant Waggit was turned all the way around, he saw that there was nothing in the room except for himself. Sergeant Waggit said to himself, "Crazy, I swear there was someone or something in the room with me." Sergeant Waggit turned around to see nothing more than a black figure standing in front of him. The figure had its back to him so that Sergeant Waggit could not see the face. Sergeant Waggit looked at the black figure and said, "Who are you?" The black figure replied to his question, "I am here to serve. You are not supposed to be here." Sergeant Waggit got impatient with this black figure and said with a more firm voice, "Like I said, Who are you? Show yourself!" The black figure turned around and looked at Sergeant Waggit in the eyes.

Sergeant Waggit looked at the black figure in the eyes as the figure turned and looked at him. He said out loud, "No! It can't be! You left! And..." The black figure then said, "Yes... I left. You remembered me as Shaft. That is not my real name though." "If that is not your real name, then what is your real name?" asked Sergeant Waggit. Shaft, the black figure, came closer to Sergeant Waggit and said, "I am the youngest daughter of Persephone and Hades. My real name is Macaria (m-aa-k-aa-r-EE-aa). I was sent here by my sister who betrayed me. I have been trapped in the Underworld of Tartarus for eternity until the realms return normal. My father does not know that I am here and my mother, queen of the underworld, thinks that I am lost. I call myself Shaft to disguise my inner beauty from everyone. This helps me hide within the walls outside my home. My true identity is being a beautiful young woman who has the look of a young teenager. My father wears black and I like to follow in his footsteps. My ego is not very frightening, however, when I wear the black cloak it shields my beauty and reveals a monster. This keeps the human race from trying to capture me when I am in the flesh. I have a duty to perform helping souls that want to live in paradise without the treacherous torture. My sister has a duty of haunting the human race and showing them how to manifest their inner dark spirits. My sister and I constantly fight about who is more beautiful and what duties we perform. My sister betrayed me by removing me from my lair of duties and sending me to this unforsaken place. I don't think she betrayed me for her inner beauty but rather for her duties as my duties are more relaxed and peaceful."

Sergeant Waggit interrupted Shaft by saying, "So, let me get this straight. Your sister betrayed you because she would rather have your job instead of hers." Shaft used her hands to create a video among a nearby wall. She looked at Sergeant Waggit and said, "Look, I will show you what happened." Sergeant Waggit turned and watched the video play among the nearby wall. He watched as Shaft's sister betrayed her within the lair of paradise trying to express her feelings about whose workload is more important. Sergeant Waggit became angry as he watched a series of amplitude events that occurred showing a battle between Shaft and her sister. He turned from the video and looked at Shaft and said, "So, you just let her overpower you and get away with it." Shaft stopped the video playback and turned towards Sergeant Waggit. She began to say, "I had no choice as she is stronger than me. I have tried to win against her battles and I fail every time. My father is proud of me for who I am but he wishes that I am to be more like my sister." Sergeant Waggit put his right hand onto his chin as he was thinking of something to say that would be nice and calm. Then after putting his hand down he began to say, "Everyone has a special ability to perform within this universe and is unique in every way. I understand where your father is coming from as my father once told me back in the day that I needed to be more like my brother as he didn't curse as much and he was more of a giving type person. I chose to be who I am and the cursing makes me unique along with my abilities to not just give everything up." Shaft held up her right hand above her head and said, "My sister is much older than me and more wise than I am. I feel as if she's towering this high and I'm just below her as a wing or something underneath her. My mother loved both of us and wished that we could get along without fighting all the time. Most of the time it's because my sister refuses to agree that I am doing my part when she needs to do her part. My sister chose to do the job she does with haunting and terrifying souls. My father gave her the option of what job she wanted and without any mercy or regret she chose to perform the haunting rather than being in paradise. When I was sent to be in paradise within the mountains, I discovered how nice it was and calm with the absence of terror and haunting. I believe that my sister is simply jealous because she made the wrong decision when choosing her duties. I don't want to harm her or my family for doing the wrong things. I just wish to have them agree to everything that I do."

Sergeant Waggit held out his left hand towards Shaft. He began to say with a calm voice, "Place your hand upon my hand and read my thoughts of how I have been over the years." As Shaft reached out towards Sergeant Waggit to place her hand onto his hand, Sergeant Waggit pulled his hand back and said, "Wait... You're not going to kill me like your father would if he was to touch somebody... right." Shaft stopped in her tracks and said, "I am nothing like my father where he can control death altogether by just a single touch and would take someone's life. I may wear his clothes but I'm sure nothing will happen to you." Sergeant Waggit then put his hand back out. Shaft placed her hand onto his hand. She began to read Sergeant Waggit's mind from his past. Shaft saw all the goodness that Sergeant Waggit had performed during his life. She also saw a dark evil side of him that was even darker than her father. Shaft didn't like what she saw but she knew that Sergeant Waggit was a good person. Shaft let go of Sergeant Waggit's hand and said, "I understand everything now. You are a good person with a good deed to serve the light and everything that you love. You do have a dark evil side too but you choose not to use it. You are like my father in a way where he desires most what he wants and right now your desire is to set balance to the universe. The stones that you seek give you the ability to set the balance with the universe between the light and the dark. You have collected all of these stones except for one of them. The last stone that you seek out is the life stone, which is the most powerful stone of all of them. The life stone has the ability to control all life whether it is dark or light." Sergeant Waggit took out his Rod of God and showed it to Shaft. He said while pointing to each stone on the rod, "Yes, I have collected eleven stones and harness their energy through this weapon. I carved slots within this rod to hold the stones in place. Eleven slots are filled up with the eleven stones that I have collected during my journey. It was not easy to relocate all the stones from when you stripped them from me the last time that we had an encounter on Earth." Shaft put both of her hands to her side and said with an outraged voice, "Back then, I had no idea who you were and what your mission was in collecting the stones that control the universe. However, now that you have let me see into your soul, I was able to see your purpose for collecting the stones. I will do whatever it takes to help you retrieve the last stone, as I know the whereabouts of its location." Sergeant Waggit looked at Shaft and said while holding both hands up as if he was going to hold something, "Wait... you know where the last stone is." Shaft turned around and began to head out of the open room. She stopped in her tracks and turned her head to the left. Shaft then said, "Well, you coming?" Sergeant Waggit put away the Rod of God and said, "Yes, right behind you." He then began to follow Shaft through the dungeon to locate the last stone.

After walking around for hours, Sergeant Waggit was getting the feeling that he was going in circles and that Shaft was taking him on a wild goose chase. Sergeant Waggit stopped walking behind Shaft and said, "Wait a minute. Where are we going? It seems like we are walking in circles as I keep seeing the same statues and figures along the walls." Shaft stopped in her tracks and turned around. She looked at Sergeant Waggit and said,

"It's just up ahead not far from this location." Sergeant Waggit got the feeling that Shaft was going to spring a trap on him. He really didn't understand her purpose of why she's here and all of a sudden why she came back. He does know however that Shaft has stolen the stones from him before and may have a plan to do it again. Sergeant Waggit kept his guard up against Shaft just in case she was to betray him just like how her sister betrayed her or that's what she says anyway. Shaft turned around and continued walking through the dungeon. Sergeant Waggit followed her through the thick walls of the dungeon with his heavy cannon rifle in his hands in the prone position. Shaft knew that Sergeant Waggit was holding a weapon in his hands and said while she was walking, "Is that necessary to hold a weapon in your hands? I assure you that you are in good hands and I am not here to betray you or anything of that matter. And I'm not here to fight you either." Sergeant Waggit then said, "Then, what is your purpose here other than what you had spoken to me about? I know you said that you are here for eternity but you're a God for a crying out loud. You have the ability to go anywhere in the universe and nothing is holding you back." Sergeant Waggit became annoyed when he did not hear a response from Shaft. He elevated his voice while he was speaking to her saying, "Tell me... Tell me now! Tell me, what is your purpose here! Why won't you answer me! Am I going to die?" Shaft stopped again and said while elevating her voice as well, "You are not going to die. I will not have that burden on my head! I will not let my father kill you! I... I!" Sergeant Waggit heard what Shaft had to say, he interrupted Shaft as she was saying the last I and said, "You what?" Shaft turned around and faced Sergeant Waggit. She then said, "I cannot speak of this to you." Sergeant Waggit became extremely upset and annoyed with her responses and he began to shout out, "You cannot speak of what! Tell me!... Fuck'n tell me now, damnit!!" Shaft drooped her right hand across Sergeant Waggit's face and said in a beautiful sweet tone, "I love you." In anger, Sergeant Waggit lashed out towards Shaft by saying, "I no you have something to tell me that is extremely important... Wait! What!?" Shaft then said again, "I love you." Sergeant Waggit looked at Shaft up and down and said with a slight excited voice, "You love me." Shaft then said with a passion from her heart, "Every since I laid my eyes upon you, I fell in love for the very first time. I have loved lots of different souls and people, however, you are the first that I have a true desire to actually love. It is as if you complete me within my family or you give me the feeling that makes me understand that I'm not alone in the universe." Sergeant Waggit put his right hand across his face and looked down, shaking his head left and right as if he just was confused or could not understand what just happened. He then looked up at Shaft and said, "Are you sure that you are absolutely speaking from your heart and not just because I have eleven stones and when I get the last stone I will then never inevitably be destroyed." Shaft put her hands across her heart as if she was holding a heart even though she did not have one physically because she was a god but still to show affection and then said, "I am truly speaking from my heart." Sergeant Waggit took a good look at the beauty within but then shook his head side to side and said, "I know that you love me but how can I show affection to you when you look like death itself when that's not what I'm all about?" Shaft used her immortal powers to transform herself from the death like figure looking similar to the grim reaper to turning into a very beautiful young woman that was dressed in tights ready to fight anything that would come her way. She looked at Sergeant Waggit and said, "This is my true identity." Sergeant Waggit had an expression on his face as if he was extremely wowed over the sight and said, "This is your true identity. You're one of the most beautiful things I've ever seen."

Shaft turned around again and continued heading through the dungeon. As she was walking, Shaft began to say, "Oh, by the way, what happens in the dungeon stays in the dungeon." Sergeant Waggit asked, "What is that supposed to mean?" Shaft replied with a smile on her face while she was walking, "I am not allowed to show my true identity outside my family home. It is forbidden and it is treason for me by showing my true identity outside. However, down here in this treacherous dungeon, my family does not know that I am here." Sergeant Waggit ran up to Shaft and put his hand out towards her in an offering for her to hold his hand. He then said with a smile on his face, "Please, take my hand and hold it as an offering to show my affection to you." Shaft reached out with her left hand as Sergeant Waggit's right hand was out and firmly grasped his hand. She then said, "This feels really nice and comforting. By the way, you can stop calling me Shaft and call me by my true name, Macaria." Sergeant Waggit looked at Shaft and said, "Okay, I will call you Macaria as long as you stay the way you are and not change back. I like this form of you a lot better as you remind me of someone that I used to know when I lived on Earth." Macaria looked at Sergeant Waggit and said, "Tell me, what was this person like, that looked like me back on Earth?" Sergeant Waggit looked at Macaria and mentioned, "Her name was Isabella. She was a beautiful young woman that loved me for who I was. She had the same body structure as yours and had a sweet young voice. I loved her before I had joined the military forces and married her after I had returned from boot camp. She bore a child of mine who grew up to be just like me. As I was done with a mission out of my country and was heading towards an organization known as NASA, Isabella was coming back from a doctor's appointment and had a car accident. I received a phone call from a paramedic as they were telling me that she did not live. At that moment I thought my life was over as the love of my life was gone forever. Later on after a crazy mission within space, I returned to find that my child raised other children that had children. When I returned to Earth, the youngest child, known as my grandson, was the same age as me which seemed so strange as it was one-hundred seventy years later after the death of my wife." Macaria looked at Sergeant Waggit and said with a tear running down her face from her left eye, "I'm so sorry to hear that. Is there anything that I can do that would help the situation?" Sergeant Waggit looked at Macaria and said, "Yes, just be beside me and that will be enough to comfort my soul." Macaria then said, "That will work with me." Sergeant Waggit and Macaria walked through the dungeon together.

After staring at the walls that were similar in almost every single room, Sergeant Waggit and Macaria reached the location of the whereabouts where the last stone was placed. Sergeant Waggit and Macaria stopped walking when they approached a room that had a statue of the beautiful woman holding her hands out as if she was cupping something within her hands. Sergeant Waggit said, "Could it be." Macaria let go of Sergeant Waggit's hand and walked over to the statue. She said while examining the statue and a glowing object within the palms of the hands, "Yes, the statue is holding the last stone. However, there is a plaque with a saying on it that says, 'To whom dares take this stone shall face severe consequences.' I think that I should grab the stone rather than you so if there is any burden upon taking the stone then it will not destroy you as I am a god it will not destroy me." With high trust in Macaria, Sergeant Waggit went ahead and said, "Go ahead and retrieve the stone for me." Macaria reached out and secured the last Stone in the grasp of her hands. She turned around and began walking towards the location where Sergeant Waggit was standing. All of a sudden a portal opened behind her. Sergeant Waggit noticed this strange portal and yelled out, "Hurry, bring the stone to me!" As the portal was open, two big hands came out of the portal and grabbed Macaria. One hand held her waist while the other hand ripped the stone out of her hands. As the hand was taking the stone and holding Macaria in place, Macaria yelled out, "My love, help me!!" The hands then released Macaria and went back into the portal. Macaria turned around as fast as she could and jumped into the portal. As Macaria was entering the portal, she yelled out, "Come back here with that stone!!" Sergeant Waggit, feeling terrified of what just happened and not knowing where the stone is now or even where this portal will lead him, he decided at the very last second as the portal was beginning to shut to run towards it. Right when the portal was almost the same size as an entry door to a house, Sergeant Waggit jumped through the portal hoping it would lead him to locating the stone that was taken and also locating his new beloved, Macaria.

CHAPTER EIGHTEEN

Lost Stone of Life

Falling through a portal with stars moving past at great speeds was a sight to see. Sergeant Waggit was glad that his suit could handle the speed that he was traveling through. It was like traveling through space faster than the speed of light with a lot of turns. Just as soon as Sergeant Waggit thought that he was done with the portal, another portal opened up sending him to another portal. He passed through twelve different portals before landing in an unknown world. After the portal jumping, Sergeant Waggit fell out of the sky and landed on his back on a hard ground just outside a strange temple. He got up and looked around to see if he may recognize the place. The temple that Sergeant Waggit landed within was unknown to his past adventures. There was a unique castle that was tall and had many towers pointing high in the sky. The entryway had a long bridge that led to the front door to the castle. Sergeant Waggit picked up all of his belongings and began heading towards the main entry door to the castle. As he got closer to the main entry door,

Sergeant Waggit noticed that there was lava spewing out of the sides of two towers like a waterfall. There was an old grandfather clock above the main entry door to the castle. Sergeant Waggit was looking at the clock as it was acting strange. He saw the hands moving fast in the counterclockwise direction, as if the time was reversing itself. Above his location on the bridge were two dragons that flew over the castle. The dragons didn't seem to bother him but they were a sight to see.

When Sergeant Waggit reached the main entry door to the castle, he grabbed the door knocker ring and was going to knock on the door. As soon as the ring came in contact with the door, the door swung wide open. Sergeant Waggit took it upon himself to walk into the castle. Again, to his knowledge, Sergeant Waggit had no idea where he was. As he passed through the front doors to the castle, the doors slammed shut as if someone shut them but there was no one there. Sergeant Waggit began walking through the castle with his heavy cannon rifle in the prone position ready for any suspicious surprises. As he was walking through the main lobby, a strange creature approached Sergeant Waggit. It looked at him and then took out a sword. The creature tried to attack him but with a few rounds shot off, the creature fell to the ground. The noise from the rifle woke up multiple creatures as Sergeant Waggit could hear multiple groans and moans coming from the walls within the castle. Sergeant Waggit saw that there were two different sets of stairs leading up the left and right wing of the castle. He decided to head up the left side and enter the left wing. When opening the door to the left wing, Sergeant Waggit noticed multiple demon-like floating ball creatures with huge teeth and drools. He took out his rocket launcher and began attacking each floating ball creature until each one fell to the ground. As he was shooting the rocket launcher, Sergeant Waggit had to dodge multiple spit blobs of drool as the creatures launched counter attacks against him. Once the creatures were out of the way and the area was cleared, Sergeant Waggit looked around for any items that he could use. He found a crate that was full of ammunition that will restock all of his weapons to the fullest capacity.

Sergeant Waggit continued walking through the left wing of the castle in the search for the last stone and his beloved. He opened another door that branched off to an unknown location. The hallway that led to the next room was full of cobwebs and bones along the floor. Rats were running all over the floor as Sergeant Waggit continued to walk down the hallway. At the end of the hallway, there was a large room that had multiple tunnels running through it. Within the large room there were a lot of cobwebs, more than the hallway. Sergeant Waggit used a knife to cut through the webs as they were in his way. Then all of a sudden some of the webs started to vibrate. A very large spider came climbing out of one of the tunnels. Quickly, Sergeant Waggit lit his torch on the flamethrower that he had and torched the spider as it came near him. Then he decided to go through each tunnel one at a time. As he was proceeding each tunnel, more spiders came out of the walls ranging from small spiders to large spiders. Along his way through the tunnels, Sergeant Waggit found multiple objects that would help him along his way. Within crates and boxes, there were lots of ammunition, health packs, and armor that would protect him from any attack of the monsters.

Sergeant Waggit fled through each tunnel until he reached a large open area that was free of cobwebs. When entering the large area, the ground began to shake as if there was a minor quake occurring. The wall in front of Sergeant Waggit crumbled exposing a dark hole. A leg from an eight-legged spider stepped out of the hole. Then a giant spider came crawling out into the large open area. The spider was huge in size and stood with an astonishing height of twenty feet. The colors of the spider were red and black as the legs in the front were more red than the back legs. The spider crouched down as it was sloped from the rear to the front. The fangs on the head were dripping with venom that can kill an elephant on a single bite. The fangs were as large as a standard elephant tusks. The body of the spider was wide and fitted similar to an egg shape. The spider had a tail with a stinger on the end similar to a scorpion. There was venom dripping from the stinger that contained acid that would melt armor. The shell of the spider was packed with armor that expelled gas emissions that were harmful if ingested. Sergeant Waggit took out his heavy cannon rifle and began to light up this magnificent creature. The spider zipped back and forth all over the room that Sergeant Waggit was standing in trying to avoid all the bullets coming in contact with its hyve. As Sergeant Waggit continued to perform his fire fight against this gigantic spider, the spider counter attacked by throwing acid at Sergeant Waggit's armor, whipping its tail around. The bullets from the heavy cannon rifle were not penetrating the hyve of the creature. Sergeant Waggit decided to harness his rifle and take out his missile launcher. He launched as many missiles as he could without destroying his armor, as the blowback would through him against the wall. After all of the rounds of ammunition were spent trying to destroy this spider, Sergeant Waggit removed the Rod of God for a final blow. He attacked the spider with a magma blast, which did nothing but drip off the creature. Sergeant Waggit saw that there was a new feature that was available to use on the rod. He activated the feature and aimed the rod directly towards the spider's head. With a single blow, the Rod of God pumped out a burst of energy that looked similar to a plasma discharge from a nuclear reactor. The burst of energy came in contact with the spider, spitting its head wide open, spewing out green spider slime guts all over the room. The spider made its last sound and then fell to the floor. After a moment of twitching, the spider came to a stop and ceased all of its movements.

Once the room was cleared from any hostile encounters, Sergeant Waggit continued his search within the left wing of the castle. In the back of the last room was a large chest that was locked with an old padlock. Sergeant Waggit took out his diamond hammer and stuck it against the lock. The blow from the hammer broke the lock causing it to shatter off the large chest. Sergeant Waggit lifted open the lid to the chest and observed what was inside. To his vision, there was a new type of armor that was made from the skin of a red dragon. Quickly, Sergeant Waggit snatched up the armor and strapped it on. He then back tracked his steps to the entrance of the left wing. After passing through the doors to the left wing, Sergeant Waggit ran down the stairs to the main lobby and then up the stairs to the right wing. He opened the door to the right wing and began heading down a long hallway. At the end of the hallway was another door that was shut. Sergeant Waggit opened up the door and saw that there was a room similar to the left wing. He embraced himself and prepared for any suspicious activity. Once again, the ground shook as if there was a tremor deep within the mountain that was within the walls of the castle. After the ground stopped shaking, the ground in front of Sergeant Waggit caved in on itself. There was a loud sound that came from the hole in the floor along with magma spitting up in the air. Then a gigantic creature came standing up within the hole in the floor. The creature was huge in size and had a giant head with large humanoid-like teeth. The creature raised its arms out of the hole and high into the air. It then smashed its hands down onto the ground trying to attack Sergeant Waggit. As the first hand was coming down, Sergeant Waggit performed a tuck and roll to maneuver away from the attack. He then took out his heavy cannon rifle and began shooting grenades at the creature. Each grenade would explode on the creature's hyve trying to penetrate through. The creature would get stunned by the grenades and fall towards the ground making its head and arms slam onto the floor within the room. Sergeant Waggit ran up to the creature and shot at the head and shoulders. After a few moments, the creature would get up and continue to make attacks against Sergeant Waggit. During its second wave of counterattacks, the creature began to lunge out magma balls towards Sergeant Waggit. Running all around, Sergeant Waggit did his best to dodge himself from the magma balls but that was not enough. He shouldered his heavy cannon rifle and took out the Rod of God. Using the power of ice, Sergeant Waggit was able to create ice mounds that would slow the magma balls down from hitting him. He then shot ice mounds towards the creatures head causing it to fall on the floor again. Sergeant Waggit ran over to the head again and took out his rocket launcher. He shot at the creature's head and shoulders for the second time. The creature was now taking a lot of damage. For the third time, the creature stood back up soaring high into the room. Then, the creature fled underneath the floor leaving some magma splashing into the air. The ground made some shaking sensation as if a small tremor was on the rise. The ground broke open just underneath Sergeant Waggit's feet forcing him to jump out of the way. One of the creature's hands came out of the hole and reached for Sergeant Waggit. Using his rocket launcher, Sergeant Waggit began to attack the hands as he was avoiding them. After dodging the hands and blasting them with multiple rockets, the creature finally gave up and fled back to the main opening in the floor. It then stood up and swung its arms with a counterattack trying to eliminate Sergeant Waggit. Using every weapon that he had, Sergeant Waggit was able to destroy the creature, sending it back to the magma below where it came from.

The right wing was now cleared from any hostile creatures and open for Sergeant Waggit to search for any clues. As he walked to the back of the room, Sergeant Waggit found another large chest that was locked. Again, he took out his diamond hammer and smashed open the lock. Sergeant Waggit then opened up the chest and observed what was inside. To his sight, he saw more medical packs and ammunition along with a map of the castle. The map disclosed the locations of all the areas that Sergeant Waggit has completed and the areas that were not cleared yet. Sergeant Waggit secured the map to the side of his utility belt and headed back towards the main entryway to the right wing. After exiting the right wing, Sergeant Waggit headed down the staircase and into the lobby. There was a set of big doors that opened up on the main ground floor between both wings. Sergeant Waggit locked and loaded all of his weapons as he began walking through the large double doors. Once passed the large double doors, the room that Sergeant Waggit entered was an open space area with shrubs everywhere. As he continued to walk through the room, little creatures lunged out at him from the shrubs. Sergeant Waggit took out his heavy cannon rifle and shot at the creatures. Each creature fell to the ground as they could not stand the chance of a bullet. After a long journey through the main castle, Sergeant Waggit came upon an open room that was similar to the dungeon that he was in previously. He encountered the same type of room that was open and had the same twelve statues on the left side of the room. Sergeant Waggit thought to himself, "What the fuck. Am I back in the dungeon." He stopped at the center of the statues and saw something different. He noticed that the statue that was in a cloak was missing a face, as if it was broken off. Sergeant Waggit looked around the floor to find the missing piece to the statue. He checked all over the room and then on a shelf nearby, stood the missing piece against a pillar. Sergeant Waggit recovered the missing piece to the statue and headed back over to the statue without a face. He carefully placed the missing piece onto the statue. There was a clunk noise and the outer statues began moving in towards the middle statues. All of the statues combined together leaving just one statue visible, the statue of a woman wearing a black cloak. The statue then began to crack and break into pieces revealing a woman in black wearing a black cloak. The woman looked at Sergeant Waggit and said, "You, stop where you are. You freed me from the curse of the treacherous Hades. I thank you for that. However, you are trespassing in my castle and I cannot allow you to pass." Sergeant Waggit looked at the woman and said, "Why can I not pass?" The woman replied with a grunt in her voice, "Because, you are not worth to be within these walls. You have to be the bloodline of Hades to embark upon these walls. For that, you shall have mercy upon your soul." The woman took out a staff that she had and prepared to fight Sergeant Waggit.

A battle between a woman from the love of the deep and Sergeant Waggit. The woman held up her staff and cast a power spell upon the room that would allow the ceiling to break apart and fall on top of Sergeant Waggit. Dodging every obstacle falling from the ceiling, Sergeant Waggit rolled left and right. He then used the Rod of God to send counterattacks towards the woman forcing her to stop her magic. The woman dropped her staff causing the magic spell to stop flourishing throughout the room. Sergeant Waggit shot out blows towards the woman with collecting the debris on the ground and launching them back at her. The debris came in contact with the woman causing her to shield her face. She then picked up her staff and created another spell within the room to change the structure around. The walls began to move from one location to another along with the floor tiles raising up and down into different locations. Sergeant Waggit carefully avoided the walls without being squished and had to play hopscotch on the floor tiles while they were moving all over the room. Some of the floor tiles had stripes on them and when Sergeant Waggit stepped on them, the tiles would make a noise and then disappear. He stepped on one of the floor tiles that were covered with stripes and began to raise Sergeant Waggit to the highest location in the room. The tile then made its sound and disappeared forcing Sergeant Waggit to fall from the ceiling. When

Sergeant Waggit fell down, he bounced off some of the other floating tiles and off one of the moving walls. His heavy cannon rifle strap got caught underneath the wall that he was against. Another wall was nearing Sergeant Waggit's location preparing to smash into the wall that his strap was stuck within. Sergeant Waggit got up and pulled on the strap as hard as he could. With seconds to spare and barely squeezing by the colliding walls, Sergeant Waggit was able to retrieve his weapon and escape the walls from smashing him. He then used the rifle to fire grenades at the woman forcing her to stop her magic. Once again, the woman dropped her staff, which in turn halted the magic from expelling from the staff. Sergeant Waggit fired all of his weapons upon the woman trying to defeat her. After a few minutes, the woman reached down and secured her staff for the third time. She cast another spell into the room causing a series of mirrors to appear. She then cast herself onto the mirrors like a fun house then yelled out, "You will never win!" Sergeant Waggit pointed his heavy cannon rifle towards each mirror and began to destroy the mirrors. Once all of the mirrors were destroyed with the exception of four mirrors, Sergeant Waggit put away his heavy cannon rifle and took out the diamond hammer. Showing his reflection in the mirror to his front may be enough of a distraction to get the woman to attack him. The woman saw Sergeant Waggit standing in the room and rushed him. She smashed into the mirror as she was trying to attach Sergeant Waggit. The woman turned around and saw Sergeant Waggit standing on the other side of the room. She rushed across the room with all her force and smashed into another mirror. Sergeant Waggit stood in front of the last two mirrors and yelled out, "Come get me!" The woman rushed to where Sergeant Waggit was standing and performed a force attack with her staff. To her surprise, she destroyed another mirror that was displaying Sergeant Waggit's reflection. Sergeant Waggit yelled out, "You missed!" The woman heard the voice of Sergeant Waggit and turned around. Standing in front of her was Sergeant Waggit. She looked down at him and tried to perform an attack, however, Sergeant Waggit beat her to the attack with a counterattack. As Sergeant Waggit was swinging his diamond hammer towards the woman's head similar to an uppercut, he yelled out, "Take this you bitch!!" The diamond hammer smashed into the head of the woman causing her to fly across the room.

Sergeant Waggit walked over to the woman as she moaned on the ground in pain. He kneeled in front of her and said, "Who are you?" With blood running out of her mouth, the woman responded, "I am the sister of Macaria. My name is Melinoe. I was sent here in flesh to vanish you from existence as I am the protector of the realm. You have proven to me that you are worthy of walking amongst the walls of my castle. However, you have not faced my father, Zeus." Sergeant Waggit interrupted the woman with saying, "Wait... I thought that Hades was your father." The woman then responded with a gasp of air as it was getting hard for her to breath in the flesh, "No, my father is not Hades. I just serve Hades and this is not his castle either." Sergeant Waggit was confused for a moment and then said, "If this is not Hades castle, then whose castle does it belong to?" The woman replied to Sergeant Waggit's question, "The castle belongs to my father, Zeus. I am the gatekeeper who watches over the castle from any hostile entries. My father Zeus is in the next room over to this room. He is here to vanish all evil within these walls. Hades have taken over the land with all of the Hayden Army Soldiers. My father can help you defeat Hades but you have to sacrifice the most that you love." Sergeant Waggit said to the woman, "What if I have no one to love?" With the last breath from the woman, she mentioned, "You know who you have to sacrifice as she loves you more than you think."

Sergeant Waggit stood up from the woman as her flesh was destroyed. He looked down at the woman and looked at the door that was located near the back of the room. Then he looked back at the woman and noticed that she was gone. Sergeant Waggit looked around to see where the body went within the room. He then stood there and thought about what the woman said and said to himself, "No... No. No, No, No, Noooo... That will not happen!" Sergeant Waggit could not bear to see his newly beloved destroyed from existence. He then said out loud, "That will not happen! This must not happen!" Sergeant Waggit then walked through the room to the back where the door is to the other room. He looked at the door and noticed that there was a key slot for a red key. Sergeant Waggit noticed that he did not possess such a key and needed to find it within the castle. He turned around and the woman's spirit was behind him. She said, "Here, you will need this to continue your journey." The woman's spirit handed Sergeant Waggit a red key. The woman spirit then vanished in sight. Sergeant Waggit turned around and ran over to the door. He inserted the key into the slot within the door and gave it a turn. The door lock released allowing Sergeant Waggit to push open the door. When the door opened up, Sergeant Waggit was shocked to see what was just on the other side of the castle. He saw all of the servants tied up and Zeus tied to a cross hanging upside down. Then with raging anger, Sergeant Waggit saw his beloved tied up in the back of the room. He noticed a creature that was standing right next to his beloved with a really long tongue. The creature then shrunk and turned into a man. The man stood by Sergeant Waggit's beloved and said staring at Sergeant Waggit, "Welcome!" Sergeant Waggit walked towards the man and said, "Who are you?" The man changed his appearance to be in black clothing with a black cloak and then said, "I am Hades. You will kneel to me." Hades lowered his hand with it out trying to for Sergeant Waggit to kneel to his feet. Sergeant Waggit then said while taking out the Rod of God, "I do not kneel to any man." Hades put his hand to his side and said, "I am no man. I am a god. You will kneel to me, serve me, and fight for me." Sergeant Waggit said with a little chuckle, "If you are a god, then you certainly need to have a better understanding of man before confronting them. We fight for each other, not for you or any other god like yourself." Hades then said as he began walking towards Sergeant Waggit, "I can show you how to serve a god that has immense powers. All I need is your staff." Sergeant Waggit gripped the Rod of God tighter and said, "You can show me the way of the god, but you cannot have my staff." Hades became relentless with the situation and elevated his voice. He stopped and said, "You will give me your staff or you will die!" Sergeant Waggit took the Rod of God and prepared for an attack and said out loud, "You will not have this staff and I am not the one who is going to be dying! I know that you have something of mine! Once I defeat you in the castle of Zeus, I will get what I have come here for!" Hades prepared for a charge and yelled out, "Ahhhh Neverrrr!!"

Hades charged Sergeant Waggit and began

fighting him in hand to hand combat. After a brutal beating from Sergeant Waggit, Hades spit out
blood from his mouth and yelled out, "You fool!!
Look what you've done!!" Hades backed up from
Sergeant Waggit and put both of his hands in the
air. He began to change himself to another entity.
After a moment, Hades turned into a giant gargoyle. The giant gargoyle roared in the room
sounding like a lion defending his territory. Sergeant Waggit took out his weapons and began to
attack the gargoyle. The gargoyle performed multiple counterattacks in an attempt to destroy Sergeant Waggit. Running all over the room, Sergeant
Waggit dodged all of the attacks from the gargoyle.
He then made the creature dizzy and fall to the
ground. Sergeant Waggit thought to himself,
"Now, this is my chance." Sergeant Waggit ran up
to the gargoyle and stabbed the Rod of God
through the heart of the beast. The gargoyle
screamed in terror and then stopped moving. Sergeant Waggit took out the Rod of God and stepped
away from the gargoyle. The creature then returned to the form of a man. The man stood up
with blood all over his body. The man said, "You
have come prepared but not good enough." The
man being Hades transformed into a giant cyclops
and trimmed a nearby tree to be a club as a
weapon. The cyclops let out a very loud roar and
began swinging the club around destroying everything in sight. Sergeant Waggit did everything
that he could to escape the deadly blows of the

club. Then when the cyclops was finally tired of swinging the club, Sergeant Waggit began attacking the creature with all of the weapons that he had. After multiple attacks, Sergeant Waggit was able to force the creature to sit down. He then took out his diamond hammer and ran up to the creature. Sergeant Waggit swung the hammer in an upward motion and then down onto the head of cyclops. The hammer smashed into the creature causing the head to fall into the spine and below the shoulders. With a final grasp of air, the creature fell silent on the floor. Sergeant Waggit watched the creature vanish and turn back into the man that first approached him as Hades. The man looked at Sergeant Waggit and said, "You have won this battle but you have not won the war." Hades then vanished from the room through the floor. A chest appeared where Hades was standing before as if magic was placing it there. Sergeant Waggit kneeled down and opened the chest. Inside the chest was the last stone that he was looking for. Sergeant Waggit put on his glove and grasped the stone into his hand. He stared at the stone for a moment and then said, "I have finally found all of the stones."

Sergeant Waggit stood up and attached the last stone to the Rod of God. A new power arises upon the rod giving it a white glowing effect. Sergeant Waggit yelled out, "Finally, I am now immortal to any god!" A voice in the background said,

"You are not immortal yet." Sergeant Waggit looked around and then said, "Who said that?" A woman approached Sergeant Waggit in a full cloak with her face hidden. She took off her hoody and looked at Sergeant Waggit. She then said, "Someone who loves you very much." Sergeant Waggit turned and saw his beloved standing next to him. He said with a smile on his face, "I... I thought that you were dead. I saw someone tied up in the back of the room but I did not know that it was you." Sergeant Waggit's beloved, Macaria, hugged him and then said, "You now need to take the rod back to your home base and give it to your leader, Cocino. He is your only hope in giving you the power that you need. He has to refine the staff into a steel that is made of pure light and melt the stones into it to forge a new weapon. Only then you will be immortal and able to destroy any god that stands up against you." Sergeant Waggit held Macaria's hands and nodded. They both turned and began to head out of the castle. As they both were leaving the castle, an army was preparing for war in the distance. Sergeant Waggit looked at Macaria and said, "What is that in the distance? Wait, is that soldiers gathering together like a formation before a massive war?" Macaria replied to his question, "They want our heads and now that you have the last stone, Hades will want to send everything at you to keep you from returning to your home base." Sergeant Waggit then said, "So, I defeated Hades and now he wants to return with his army to fight me again." Macaria turned to Sergeant Waggit and said, "I know it will be tough, but this time you will have me to help you fight and win against Hades and his army that he calls, the Hyadeans." Sergeant Waggit then said, "Even though you are his child, he wants your head too." Macaria nodded and replied, "I betrayed his trust by showing my true identity outside my home. My father will not let me return to the mountains unless I can show him that I am worth to serve by his side once again." Sergeant Waggit looked at Macaria and took out his heavy cannon rifle. Macaria activated her powers to prepare for war. Sergeant Waggit then said to Macaria, "Okay, let's go win this war and show your father that you do matter." Sergeant Waggit and Macaria began heading down a path towards the armies in a distant land far away.

ABOUT THE AUTHOR

Marvin Sunderland

 Marvin Sunderland is a dynamic author and philosopher of natural space phenomenon analogies and extraterrestrial design. Sunderland has spent countless days gazing upon the stars looking for life beyond our own existance. With writing for science fiction, Sunderland also intended to use real events that currently uplift scientists creativity of understanding how the universe works. To this day, Sunderland knows that with the vastness of space and the universe expanding at a presented rate, the understanding of the human race being alone is not accurate by defination. Sunderland intended to use his findings to impress readers and show them that we are not alone in this universe.

Made in the USA
Middletown, DE
03 June 2023

32021277R00163